Rachel Ray
Vol. II

by

Anthony Trollope

Rachel Ray
Vol. II
by Anthony Trollope

ISBN: 978-93-64285-93-3

Published by

DOUBLE 9 BOOKS

2/13-B, Ansari Road
Daryaganj, New Delhi – 110002
info@double9books.com
www.double9books.com
Tel. 011-40042856

This book is under public domain

ABOUT THE AUTHOR

Anthony Trollope (1815-1882) was a renowned English novelist of the Victorian era, best known for his insightful and richly detailed portrayals of 19th-century English society. His prolific writing career produced a vast array of novels, many of which have become classics of English literature. First Novels: Trollope's debut novel, "The Macdermots of Ballycloran", was published in 1847. However, it was not until the publication of "The Warden" in 1855 that he gained significant recognition. Trollope's writing is known for its realism, detailed character development, and exploration of social issues. His characters are often complex and multifaceted, reflecting the diverse nature of human experiences. He employed a straightforward narrative style, often interjecting his own commentary and opinions, which adds a distinctive voice to his works. Trollope's works remain significant in the study of Victorian literature. His keen observations of society, human relationships, and institutional behaviors continue to be appreciated for their depth and insight. Many of his novels have been adapted for television, radio, and stage, keeping his stories and characters alive for new generations. Anthony Trollope's contribution to literature is marked by his ability to combine detailed social critique with engaging storytelling, making him one of the enduring figures of English literature.

CONTENTS

CHAPTER I
RACHEL RAY'S FIRST LOVE-LETTER

On the Monday evening, after tea, Mrs. Prime came out to the cottage. It was that Monday on which Mrs. Rowan and her daughter had left Baslehurst and had followed Luke up to London. She came out and sat with her mother and sister for about an hour, restraining herself with much discretion from the saying of disagreeable things about her sister's lover. She had heard that the Rowans had gone away, and she had also heard that it was probable that they would be no more seen in Baslehurst. Mr. Prong had given it as his opinion that Luke would not trouble them again by his personal appearance among them. Under these circumstances Mrs. Prime had thought that she might spare her sister. Nor had she said much about her own love affairs. She had never mentioned Mr. Prong's offer in Rachel's presence; nor did she do so now. As long as Rachel remained in the room the conversation was very innocent and very uninteresting. For a few minutes the two widows were alone together, and then Mrs. Prime gave her mother to understand that things were not yet quite arranged between herself and Mr. Prong.

"You see, mother," said Mrs. Prime, "as this money has been committed to my charge, I do not think it can be right to let it go altogether out of my own hands."

In answer to this Mrs. Ray had uttered a word or two agreeing with her daughter. She was afraid to say much against Mr. Prong;—was afraid, indeed, to express any very strong opinion about this proposed marriage; but in her heart she would have been delighted to hear that the Prong alliance was to be abandoned. There was nothing in Mr. Prong to recommend him to Mrs. Ray.

"And is she going to marry him?" Rachel asked, as soon as her sister was gone.

"There's nothing settled as yet. Dorothea wants to keep her money in her own hands."

"I don't think that can be right. If a woman is married the money should belong to the husband."

"I suppose that's what Mr. Prong thinks;—at any rate, there's nothing settled. It seems to me that we know so little about him. He might go away any day to Australia, you know."

"And did she say anything about—Mr. Rowan?"

"Not a word, my dear."

And that was all that was then said about Luke even between Rachel and her mother. How could they speak about him? Mrs. Ray also believed that he would be no more seen in Baslehurst; and Rachel was well aware that such was her mother's belief, although it had never been expressed. What could be said between them now,—or ever afterwards,—unless, indeed, Rowan should take some steps to make it necessary that his doings should be discussed?

The Tuesday passed and the Wednesday, without any sign from the young man; and during these two sad days nothing was said at the cottage. On that Wednesday his name was absolutely not mentioned between them, although each of them was thinking of him throughout the day. Mrs. Ray had now become almost sure that he had obeyed his mother's behests, and had resolved not to trouble himself about Rachel any further; and Rachel herself had become frightened if not despondent. Could it be that all this should have passed over her and that it should mean nothing?—that the man should have been standing there, only three or four days since, in that very room, with his arm round her waist, begging for her love, and calling her his wife;—and that all of it should have no meaning? Nothing amazed her so much as her mother's firm belief in such an ending to such an affair. What must be her mother's thoughts about men and women in general if she could expect such conduct from Luke Rowan,—and yet not think of him as one whose falsehood was marvellous in its falseness!

But on the Thursday morning there came a letter from Luke addressed to Rachel. On that morning Mrs. Ray was up when the postman passed by the cottage, and though Rachel took the letter from the man's hand herself, she did not open it till she had shown it to her mother.

"Of course it's from him," said Rachel.

"I suppose so," said Mrs. Ray, taking the unopened letter in her hand and looking at it. She spoke almost in a whisper, as though there were something terrible in the coming of the letter.

"Is it not odd," said Rachel, "but I never saw his handwriting before? I shall know it now for ever and ever." She also spoke in a whisper, and still held the letter as though she dreaded to open it.

"Well, my dear," said Mrs. Ray.

"If you think you ought to read it first, mamma, you may."

"No, Rachel. It is your letter. I do not wish you to imagine that I distrust you."

Then Rachel sat herself down, and with extreme care opened the envelope. The letter, which she read to herself very slowly, was as follows:—

> My own dearest Rachel,
>
> It seems so nice having to write to you, though it would be much nicer if I could see you and be sitting with you at this moment at the churchyard stile. That is the spot in all Baslehurst that I like the best. I ought to have written sooner, I know, and you will have been very angry with me; but I have had to go down into Northamptonshire to settle some affairs as to my father's property, so that I have been almost living in railway carriages ever since I saw you. I am resolved about the brewery business more firmly than ever, and as it seems that "T"

—Mrs. Tappitt would occasionally so designate her lord, and her doing so had been a joke between Luke and Rachel,—

> will not come to reason without a lawsuit, I must scrape together all the capital I have, or I shall be fifty years old before I can begin. He is a pig-headed old fool, and I shall be driven to ruin him and all his family. I would have done,— and still would do,—anything for him in kindness; but if he drives me to go to law to get what is as much my own as his share is his own, I will build another brewery just under his nose. All this will require money, and therefore I have to run about and get my affairs settled.
>
> But this is a nice love-letter,—is it not? However, you must take me as I am. Just now I have beer in my very soul. The grand object of my ambition is to stand and be fumigated by the smoke of my own vats. It is a fat, prosperous, money-making business, and one in which there is a clear line between right and wrong. No man brews bad beer without knowing it,—or sells short measure. Whether the fatness and the honesty can go together;—that is the problem I want to solve.

You see I write to you exactly as if you were a man friend, and not my own dear sweet girl. But I am a very bad hand at love-making. I considered that that was all done when you nodded your head over my arm in token that you consented to be my wife. It was a very little nod, but it binds you as fast as a score of oaths. And now I think I have a right to talk to you about all my affairs, and expect you at once to get up the price of malt and hops in Devonshire. I told you, you remember, that you should be my friend, and now I mean to have my own way.

You must tell me exactly what my mother has been doing and saying at the cottage. I cannot quite make it out from what she says, but I fear that she has been interfering where she had no business, and making a goose of herself. She has got an idea into her head that I ought to make a good bargain in matrimony, and sell myself at the highest price going in the market;—that I ought to get money, or if not money, family connexion. I'm very fond of money,—as is everybody, only people are such liars,—but then I like it to be my own; and as to what people call connexion, I have no words to tell you how I despise it. If I know myself I should never have chosen a woman as my companion for life who was not a lady; but I have not the remotest wish to become second cousin by marriage to a baronet's grandmother. I have told my mother all this, and that you and I have settled the matter together; but I see that she trusts to something that she has said or done herself to upset our settling. Of course, what she has said can have no effect on you. She has a right to speak to me, but she ha_s none to speak to you;—not as yet. But she is the best woman in the world, and as soon as ever we are married you will find that she will receive you with open arms.

You know I spoke of our being married in August. I wish it could have been so. If we could have settled it when I was at Bragg's End, it might have been done. I don't, however, mean to scold you, though it was your fault. But as it is, it must now be put off till after Christmas. I won't name a day yet for seeing you, because I couldn't well go to Baslehurst without putting myself into Tappitt's way. My lawyer says I had better not go to Baslehurst just at present. Of course you will write to me constantly,—to my address here; say, twice a week at least. And I shall expect you to tell me everything that goes on. Give my kind love to your mother.

Yours, dearest Rachel,
Most affectionately,

Luke Rowan.

The letter was not quite what Rachel had expected, but, nevertheless, she thought it very nice. She had never received a love-letter before, and probably had never read one,—even in print; so that she was in possession of no strong preconceived notions as to the nature or requisite contents of such a document. She was a little shocked when Luke called his mother a goose;—she was a little startled when he said that people were "liars," having an idea that the word was one not to be lightly used;—she was amused by the allusion to the baronet's grandmother, feeling, however, that the manner and language of his letter was less pretty and love-laden than she had expected;—and she was frightened when he so confidently called upon her to write to him twice a week. But, nevertheless, the letter was a genial one, joyous, and, upon the whole, comforting. She read it very slowly, going back over much of it twice and thrice, so that her mother became impatient before the perusal was finished.

"It seems to be very long," said Mrs. Ray.

"Yes, mamma, it is long. It's nearly four sides."

"What can he have to say so much?"

"There's a good deal of it is about his own private affairs."

"I suppose, then, I mustn't see it."

"Oh yes, mamma!" And Rachel handed her the letter. "I shouldn't think of having a letter from him and not showing it to you;—not as things are now." Then Mrs. Ray took the letter and spent quite as much time in reading it as Rachel had done. "He writes as though he meant to have everything quite his own way," said Mrs. Ray.

"That's what he does mean. I think he will do that always. He's what people call imperious; but that isn't bad in a man, is it?"

Mrs. Ray did not quite know whether it was bad in a man or no. But she mistrusted the letter, not construing it closely so as to discover what might really be its full meaning, but perceiving that the young man took, or intended to take, very much into his own hands; that he demanded that everything should be surrendered to his will and pleasure, without any guarantee on his part that such surrendering should be properly acknowledged. Mrs. Ray was disposed to doubt people and things that were at a distance from her. Some check could be kept over a lover at Baslehurst; or, if perchance the lover had removed himself only to Exeter, with which city Mrs. Ray was personally acquainted, she could have believed in his return. He would not, in that case, have gone utterly beyond her ken. But she could put no confidence in a lover up in London. Who could say that he might not marry some one else to-morrow,—that he might not be promising to marry half a dozen? It was with her the same sort of feeling which made her think it possible that Mr. Prong might go to Australia. She would have liked as a lover for her daughter a young man fixed in business,—if not at Baslehurst, then at Totnes, Dartmouth, or Brixham,—under her own eye as it were;—a young man so fixed that all the world of South Devonshire would know of all his doings. Such a young man, when he asked a girl to marry him, must mean what he said. If he did not there would be no escape for him from the punishment of his neighbours' eyes and tongues. But a young man up in London,—a young man who had quarrelled with his natural friends in Baslehurst,—a young man who was confessedly masterful and impetuous,—a young man who called his own mother a goose, and all the rest of the world liars, in his first letter to his lady-love;—was that a young man in whom Mrs. Ray could place confidence as a lover for her pet lamb? She read the letter very slowly, and then, as she gave it back to Rachel, she groaned.

For nearly half an hour after that nothing was said in the cottage about the letter. Rachel had perceived that it had not been thought satisfactory by her mother; but then she was inclined to believe that her mother would have regarded no letter as satisfactory until arguments had been used to prove to her that it was so. This, at any rate, was clear,—must be clear to Mrs. Ray as it was clear to Rachel,—that Luke had no intention of shirking the fulfilment of his engagement. And after all, was not that the one thing as to which it was essentially necessary that they should be confident? Had she not accepted Luke, telling him that she loved him? and was it not acknowledged by all around her that such a marriage would be good for her? The danger which they feared was the expectation of such a marriage without its accomplishment. Even the forebodings of Mrs. Prime had shown that this was the evil to which they pointed. Under these circumstances what better could be wished for than a ready, quick, warm assurance on Luke's part, that he did intend all that he had said?

With Rachel now, as with all girls under such circumstances, the chief immediate consideration was as to the answer which should be given. Was she to write to him, to write what she pleased; and might she write at once? She felt that she longed to have the pen in her hand, and that yet, when holding it, she would have to think for hours before writing the first word. "Mamma," she said at last, "don't you think it's a good letter?"

"I don't know what to think, my dear. I doubt whether any letters of that sort are good for much."

"Of what sort, mamma?"

"Letters from men who call themselves lovers to young girls. It would be safer, I think, that there shouldn't be any;—very much safer."

"But if he hadn't written we should have thought that he had forgotten all about us. That would not have been good. You said yourself that if he did not write soon, there would be an end of everything."

"A hundred years ago there wasn't all this writing between young people, and these things were managed better then than they are now, as far as I can understand."

"People couldn't write so much then," said Rachel, "because there were no railways and no postage stamps. I suppose I must answer it, mamma?" To this proposition Mrs. Ray made no immediate answer. "Don't you think I ought to answer it, mamma?"

"You can't want to write at once."

"In the afternoon would do."

"In the afternoon! Why should you be in so much hurry, Rachel? It took him four or five days to write to you."

"Yes; but he was down in Northamptonshire on business. Besides he hadn't any letter from me to answer. I shouldn't like him to think—"

"To think what, Rachel?"

"That I had forgotten him."

"Psha!"

"Or that I didn't treat his letter with respect."

"He won't think that. But I must turn it over in my mind; and I believe I ought to ask somebody."

"Not Dolly," said Rachel, eagerly.

"No, not your sister. I will not ask her. But if you don't mind, my dear, I'll take the young man's letter out to Mr. Comfort, and consult him. I never felt myself so much in need of somebody to advise me. Mr. Comfort is an old man, and you won't mind his seeing the letter."

Rachel did mind it very much, but she had no means of saving herself from her fate. She did not like the idea of having her love-letter submitted to the clergyman of the parish. I do not know any young lady who would have liked it. But bad as that was, it was preferable to having the letter submitted to Mrs. Prime. And then she remembered that Mr. Comfort had advised that she might go to the ball, and that he was father to her friend Mrs. Butler Cornbury.

CHAPTER II
ELECTIONEERING

And now, in these days,—the days immediately following the departure of Luke Rowan from Baslehurst,—the Tappitt family were constrained to work very hard at the task of defaming the young man who had lately been living with them in their house. They were constrained to do this by the necessities of their position; and in doing so by no means showed themselves to be such monsters of iniquity as the readers of the story will feel themselves inclined to call them. As for Tappitt himself, he certainly believed that Rowan was so base a scoundrel that no evil words against him could be considered as malicious or even unnecessary. Is it not good to denounce a scoundrel? And if the rascality of any rascal be specially directed against oneself and one's own wife and children, is it not a duty to denounce that rascal, so that his rascality may be known and thus made of no effect? When Tappitt declared in the reading-room at the Dragon, and afterwards in the little room inside the bar at the King's Head, and again to a circle of respectable farmers and tradesmen in the Corn Market, that young Rowan had come down to the brewery and made his way into the brewery-house with a ready prepared plan for ruining him—him, the head of the firm,—he thought that he was telling the truth. And again, when he spoke with horror of Rowan's intention of setting up an opposition brewery, his horror was conscientious. He believed that it would be very wicked in a man to oppose the Bungall establishment with money left by Bungall,—that it would be a wickedness than which no commercial rascality could be more iniquitous. His very soul was struck with awe at the idea. That anything was due in the matter to the consumer of beer, never occurred to him. And it may also be said in Tappitt's favour that his opinion,—as a general opinion,—was backed by those around him. His neighbours could not be made to hate Rowan as he hated him. They would not declare the young man to be the very Mischief, as he did. But that idea of a rival brewery was distasteful to them all. Most of them knew that the beer was almost too bad to be swallowed; but they thought that Tappitt had a vested interest in the manufacture of bad beer;—that as a manufacturer of bad beer he was a fairly honest and useful man;—and they looked upon any change as the work, or rather the suggestion, of a charlatan.

"This isn't Staffordshire," they said. "If you want beer like that you can buy it in bottles at Griggs'."

"He'll soon find where he'll be if he tries to undersell me," said young Griggs. "All the same, I hope he'll come back, because he has left a little bill at our place."

And then to other evil reports was added that special evil report,—that Rowan had gone away without paying his debts. I am inclined to think that Mr. Tappitt can be almost justified in his evil thoughts and his evil words.

I cannot make out quite so good a case for Mrs. Tappitt and her two elder daughters;—for even Martha, Martha the just, shook her head in these days when Rowan's name was mentioned;—but something may be said even for them. It must not be supposed that Mrs. Tappitt's single grievance was her disappointment as regarded Augusta. Had there been no Augusta on whose behalf a hope had been possible, the predilection of the young moneyed stranger for such a girl as Rachel Ray would have been a grievance to such a woman as Mrs. Tappitt. Had she not been looking down on Rachel Ray and despising her for the last ten years? Had she not been wondering among her friends, with charitable volubility, as to what that poor woman at Bragg's End was to do with her daughter? Had she not been regretting that the young girl should be growing up so big, and promising to look so coarse? Was it not natural that she should be miserable when she saw her taken in hand by Mrs. Butler Cornbury, and made the heroine at her own party, to the detriment of her own daughters, by the fashionable lady in catching whom she had displayed so much unfortunate ingenuity? Under such circumstances how could she do other than hate Luke Rowan,—than believe him to be the very Mischief,—than prophesying all manner of bad things for Rachel,—and assist her husband tooth and nail in his animosity against the sinner?

Augusta was less strong in her feelings than her parents, but of course she disliked the man who could admire Rachel Ray. As regards Martha, her dislike to him,—or rather, her judicial disapproval,—was founded on his social and commercial improprieties. She understood that he had threatened her father about the business,—and she had been scandalized in that matter of the champagne. Cherry was very brave, and still stood up for him before her mother and sisters;—but even Cherry did not dare to say a word in his favour before her father. Mr. Tappitt had been driven to forget himself, and to take a poker in his hand as a weapon of violence! After that let no one speak a word on the offender's behalf in Tappitt's house and within Tappitt's hearing!

In that affair of the champagne Rowan was most bitterly injured. He had ordered it, if not at the request, at least at the instigation of Mrs. Tappitt;—and he had paid for it. When he left Baslehurst he owed no shilling to any man in it; and, indeed, he was a man by no means given to owing money to any one. He was of a spirit masterful, self-confident, and perhaps self-glorious;—but he was at the same time honest and independent. That wine had been ordered in some unusual way,—not at the regular counter, and in the same way the bill for it had been paid. Griggs, when he made his assertion in the bar-room at the King's Head, had stated what he believed to be the truth. The next morning he chanced to hear that the account had been settled, but not, at the moment, duly marked off the books. As far as Griggs went that was the end of it. He did not again say that Rowan owed money to him; but he never contradicted his former assertion, and allowed the general report to go on,—that report which had been founded on his own first statement. Thus before Rowan had been a week out of the place it was believed all over the town that he had left unpaid bills behind him.

"I am told that young man is dreadfully in debt," said Mr. Prong to Mrs. Prime. At this time Mr. Prong and Mrs. Prime saw each other daily, and were affectionate in their intercourse,—with a serious, solemn affection; but affairs were by no means settled between them. That affection was, however, strong enough to induce Mr. Prong to take a decided part in opposing the Rowan alliance. "They say he owes money all over the town."

"So Miss Pucker tells me," said Mrs. Prime.

"Does your mother know it?"

"Mother never knows anything that other people know. But he has gone now, and I don't suppose we shall hear of him or see him again."

"He has not written to her, Dorothea?"

"Not that I know of."

"You should find out. You should not leave them in this danger. Your mother is weak, and you should give her the aid of your strength. The girl is your sister, and you should not leave her to grope in darkness. You should remember, Dorothea, that you have a duty in this matter."

Dorothea did not like being told of her duty in so pastoral a manner, and resolved to be more than ever particular in the protection of her own pecuniary rights before she submitted herself to Mr. Prong's marital authority once and for ever. By Miss Pucker she was at any rate treated with great respect, and was allowed perhaps some display of pastoral manner on her own part. It began to be with her a matter of doubt whether she might not be of more use in that free vineyard which she was about to leave, than in that vineyard with closed doors and a pastoral overseer, which she was preparing herself to enter. At any rate she would be careful about the money. But, in the mean time, she did agree with Mr. Prong that Rowan's proper character should be made known to her mother, and with this view she went out to the cottage and whispered into Mrs. Ray's astonished ears the fact that Luke was terribly in debt.

"You don't say so!"

"But I do say so, mother. Everybody in Baslehurst is talking about it. And they all say that he has treated Mr. Tappitt shamefully. Has anything come from him since he went?"

Then Mrs. Ray told her elder daughter of the letter, and told her also that she intended to consult Mr. Comfort. "Oh, Mr. Comfort!" said Mrs. Prime, signifying her opinion that her mother was going to a very poor counsellor. "And what sort of a letter was it?" said Mrs. Prime, with a not unnatural desire to see it.

"It was an honest letter enough,—very honest to my thinking; and speaking as though everything between them was quite settled."

"That's nonsense, mother."

"Perhaps it may be nonsense, Dorothea; but I am only telling you what the letter said. He called his mother a goose; that was the worst thing in it."

"You cannot expect that such a one as he should honour his parents."

"But his mother thinks him the finest young man in the world. And I must say this for him, that he has always spoken of her as though he loved her very dearly; and I believe he has been a most excellent son. He shouldn't have said goose;—at any rate in a letter;—not to my way of thinking. But perhaps they don't mind those things up in London."

"I never knew a young man so badly spoken of at a place he'd left as he is in Baslehurst. I think it right to tell you; but if you have made up your mind to ask Mr. Comfort—"

"Yes; I have made up my mind to ask Mr. Comfort. He has sent to say he will call the day after to-morrow." Then Mrs. Prime went back home, having seen neither the letter nor her sister.

It may be remembered that an election was impending over the town of Baslehurst, the coming necessities of which had induced Mrs. Butler Cornbury to grace Mrs. Tappitt's ball. It was now nearly the end of July, and the election was to be made early in September. Both candidates were already in the field, and the politicians of the neighbourhood already knew to a nicety how the affair would go. Mr. Hart the great clothier from Houndsditch and Regent Street, — Messrs. Hart and Jacobs of from 110 to 136 Houndsditch, and about as many more numbers in Regent Street, — would come in at the top of the poll with 173 votes, and Butler Cornbury, whose forefathers had lived in the neighbourhood for the last four hundred years and been returned for various places in Devonshire to dozens of parliaments, would be left in the lurch with 171 votes. A petition might probably unseat the Jew clothier; but then, as was well known, the Cornbury estate could not bear the expenditure of the necessary five thousand pounds for the petition, in addition to the twelve hundred which the election itself was computed to cost. It was all known and thoroughly understood; and men in Baslehurst talked about the result as though the matter were past a doubt. Nevertheless there were those who were ready to bet on the Cornbury side of the question.

But though the thing was thus accurately settled, and though its termination was foreseen by so many and with so perfect a certainty, still the canvassing went on. In fact there were votes that had not even yet been asked, much less promised, — and again, much less purchased. The Hart people were striving to frighten the Cornbury people out of the field by the fear of the probable expenditure; and had it not been for the good courage of Mrs. Butler Cornbury would probably have succeeded in doing so. The old squire was very fidgety about the money, and the young squire declared himself unwilling to lean too heavily upon his father. But the lady of the household declared her conviction that there was more smoke than fire, and more threats of bribery than intention of bribing. She would go on, she declared; and as her word passed for much at Cornbury Grange, the battle was still to be fought.

Among the votes which certainly had not as yet been promised was that of Mr. Tappitt. Mr. Hart in person had called upon him, but had not been quite satisfied with his reception. Mr. Tappitt was a man who thought much of his local influence and local privileges, and was by no means disposed to make a promise of his vote on easy terms, at a moment when his vote was becoming of so much importance. He was no doubt a liberal as was also Mr. Hart; but in small towns politics become split, and a man is not always bound to vote for a liberal candidate because he is a liberal himself. Mr. Hart had been confident in his tone, and had not sufficiently freed himself from all outer taint of his ancient race to please Mr. Tappitt's taste. "He's an impudent low Jew," he had said to his wife. "As for Butler Cornbury he gives himself airs, and is too grand even to come and ask. I don't think I shall vote at all." His wife had reminded him how civil to them Mrs. Cornbury had been;—this was before the morning of the poker;—but Tappitt had only sneered, and declared he was not going to send a man to Parliament because his wife had come to a dance.

But we, who know Tappitt best, may declare now that his vote was to have been had by any one who would have joined him energetically in abuse of Luke Rowan. His mind was full of his grievance. His heart was laden with hatred of his enemy. His very soul was heavy with that sorrow. Honyman, whom he had not yet dared to desert, had again recommended submission to him, submission to one of the three terms proposed. Let him take the thousand a year and go out from the brewery. That was Honyman's first advice. If not that, then let him admit his enemy to a full partnership. If that were too distasteful to be possible, then let him raise ten thousand pounds on a mortgage on the whole property, and buy Rowan out. Honyman thought that the money might be raised if Tappitt were willing to throw into the lump the moderate savings of his past life. But in answer to either proposal Tappitt only raved. Had Mr. Hart known all about this, he might doubtless have secured Tappitt's vote.

Butler Cornbury refused to call at the brewery. "The man's a liberal," he said to his wife, "and what's the use? Besides he's just the man I can't stand. We've always hated each other."

Whereupon Mrs. B. Cornbury determined to call on Mrs. Tappitt, and to see Tappitt himself if it were possible. She had heard something of the Rowan troubles, but not all. She had heard, too, of Rowan's liking for Rachel Ray, having also seen something of it, as we know. But, unfortunately for her husband's parliamentary interests, she had not learned that the two things were connected together. And, very unfortunately also for the same interests, she had taken it into her head that Rachel should be married to young Rowan. She had conceived a liking for Rachel; and being by nature busy, fond of employment, and apt at managing other people's affairs, she had put her finger on that match as one which she would task herself to further. This, I say, was unfortunate as regards her husband's present views. Her work, now in hand, was to secure Tappitt's vote; and to have carried her point in that quarter, her surest method would have been to have entered the brewery open-mouthed against Luke Rowan and Rachel Ray.

But the conversation, almost at once, led to a word in praise of Rachel, and to following words in praise of Luke. Martha only was in the room with her mother. Mrs. Cornbury did not at once begin about the vote, but made, as was natural, certain complimentary speeches about the ball. Really she didn't remember when she had seen anything better done; and the young ladies looked so nice. She had indeed gone away early; but she had done so by no means on her own account, but because Rachel Ray had been tired. Then she said a nice good-natured genial word or two about Rachel Ray and her performance on that occasion. "It seemed to me," she added, "that a certain young gentleman was quite smitten."

Then Mrs. Tappitt's brow became black as thunder, and Mrs. Cornbury knew at once that she had trodden on unsafe ground,—on ground which she should specially have avoided.

"We are all aware," Mrs. Tappitt said, "that the certain young gentleman behaved very badly,—disgracefully, I may say;—but it wasn't our fault, Mrs. Cornbury."

"Upon my word, Mrs. Tappitt, I didn't see anything amiss."

"I'm afraid everybody saw it. Indeed, everybody has been talking of it ever since. As regards him, what he did then was only of a piece with his general conduct, which it doesn't become me to name in the language which it deserves. His behaviour to Mr. T. has been shameful;—quite shameful."

"I had heard something, but I did not know there was anything like that. I'm so sorry I mentioned his name."

"He has disagreed with papa about the brewery business," said Martha.

"It's more than that, Martha, as you know very well," continued Mrs. Tappitt, still speaking in her great heat. "He has shown himself bad in every way,—giving himself airs all over the town, and then going away without paying his debts."

"I don't think we know that, mamma."

"Everybody says-so. Your own father heard Sam Griggs say with his own ears that there was a shop bill left there of I don't know how long. But that's nothing to us. He came here under false pretences, and now he's been turned out, and we don't want to have any more to do with him. But, Mrs. Cornbury, I am sorry about that poor foolish girl."

"I didn't think her poor or foolish at all," said Mrs. Cornbury, who had quite heart enough to forget the vote her husband wanted in her warmth for her young friend.

"I must say, then, I did;—I thought her very foolish, and I didn't at all like the way she went on in my house and before my girls. And as for him, he doesn't think of her any more than he thinks of me. In the first place, he's engaged to another girl."

"We are not quite sure that he's engaged, mamma," said Martha.

"I don't know what you call being sure, my dear. I can't say I've ever heard it sworn to, on oath. But his sister Mary told your sister Augusta that he was. I think that's pretty good evidence. But, Mrs. Cornbury, he's one of those that will be engaged to twenty, if he can find twenty foolish enough to listen to him. And for her, who never was at a dance before, to go on with him like that;—I must say that I thought it disgraceful!"

"Well, Mrs. Tappitt," said Mrs. Cornbury, speaking with much authority in her voice, "I can only say that I didn't see it. She was under my charge, and if it was as you say I must be very much to blame,—very much indeed."

"I'm sure I didn't mean that," said Mrs. Tappitt, frightened.

"I don't suppose you did,—but I mean it. As for the young gentleman, I know very little about him. He may be everything that is bad."

"You'll find that he is, Mrs. Cornbury."

"But as to Miss Ray, whom I've known all my life, and whose mother my father has known for all her life, I cannot allow anything of the kind to be said. She was under my charge; and when young ladies are under my charge I keep a close eye upon them,—for their own comfort's sake. I know how to manage for them, and I always look after them. On the night of your party I saw nothing in Miss Ray's conduct that was not nice, ladylike, and well-behaved. I must say so; and if I hear a whisper to the contrary in any quarter, you may be sure that I shall say so open-mouthed. How d'you do, Mr. Tappitt? I'm so glad you've come in, as I specially wanted to see you." Then she shook hands with Mr. Tappitt, who entered the room at the moment, and the look and manner of her face was altered.

Mrs. Tappitt was cowed. If her husband had not come in at that moment she might have said a word or two in her own defence, being driven to do so by the absence of any other mode of retreating. But as he came in so opportunely, she allowed his coming to cover her defeat. Strong as was her feeling on the subject, she did not dare to continue her attack upon Rachel in opposition to the defiant bravery which came full upon her from Mrs. Cornbury's eyes. The words had been bad, but the determined fire of those eyes had been worse. Mrs. Tappitt was cowed, and allowed Rachel's name to pass away without further remark.

Mrs. Cornbury saw it all at a glance;—saw it all and understood it. The vote was probably lost; but it would certainly be lost if Tappitt and his wife discussed the matter before he had pledged himself. The vote would probably be lost, even though Tappitt should, in his ignorance of what had just passed, pledge himself to give it. All that Mrs. Cornbury perceived, and knew that she could lose nothing by an immediate request.

"Mr. Tappitt," said she, "I have come canvassing. The fact is this: Mr. Cornbury says you are a liberal, and that therefore he has not the face to ask you. I tell him that I think you would rather support a neighbour from the county, even though there may be a shade of difference in politics between you, than a stranger, whose trade and religion cannot possibly recommend him, and whose politics, if you really knew them, would probably be quite as much unlike your own as are my husband's."

The little speech had been prepared beforehand, but was brought out quite as naturally as though Mrs. Cornbury had been accustomed to speak on her legs for a quarter of a century.

Mr. Tappitt grunted. The attack came upon him so much by surprise that he knew not what else to do but to grunt. If Mr. Cornbury had come with the same speech in his mouth, and could then have sided off into some general abuse of Luke Rowan, the vote would have been won.

"I'm sure Mrs. Tappitt will agree with me," said Mrs. Cornbury, smiling very sweetly upon the foe she had so lately vanquished.

"Women don't know anything about it," said Tappitt, meaning to snub no one but his own wife, and forgetting that Mrs. Cornbury was a woman. He blushed fiery red when the thought flashed upon him, and wished that his own drawing-room floor would open and receive him; nevertheless he was often afterwards heard to boast how he had put down the politician in petticoats when she came electioneering to the brewery.

"Well, that is severe," said Mrs. Cornbury, laughing.

"Oh, T.! you shouldn't have said that before Mrs. Cornbury!"

"I only meant my own wife, ma'am; I didn't indeed."

"I'll forgive your satire if you'll give me your vote," said Mrs. Cornbury, with her sweetest smile. "He owes it me now; doesn't he, Mrs. Tappitt?"

"Well,—I really think he do." Mrs. Tappitt, in her double trouble,—in her own defeat and her shame on behalf of her husband's rudeness,—was driven back, out of all her latter-day conventionalities, into the thoughts and even into the language of old days. She was becoming afraid of Mrs.

Cornbury, and submissive, as of old, to the rank and station of Cornbury Grange. In her terror she was becoming a little forgetful of niceties learned somewhat late in life. "I really think he do," said Mrs. Tappitt.

Tappitt grunted again.

"It's a very serious thing," he said.

"So it is," said Mrs. Cornbury, interrupting him. She knew that her chance was gone if the man were allowed to get himself mentally upon his legs. "It is very serious; but the fact that you are still in doubt shows that you have been thinking of it. We all know how good a churchman you are, and that you would not willingly send a Jew to Parliament."

"I don't know," said Tappitt. "I'm not for persecuting even the Jews;—not when they pay their way and push themselves honourably in commerce."

"Oh, yes; commerce! There is nobody who has shown himself more devoted to the commercial interests than Mr. Cornbury. We buy everything in Baslehurst. Unfortunately our people won't drink beer because of the cider."

"Tappitt doesn't think a bit about that, Mrs. Cornbury."

"I'm afraid I shall be called upon in honour to support my party," said Tappitt.

"Exactly; but which is your party? Isn't the Protestant religion of your country your party? These people are creeping down into all parts of the kingdom, and where shall we be if leading men like you think more of shades of difference between liberal and conservative than of the fundamental truths of the Church of England? Would you depute a Jew to get up and speak your own opinions in your own vestry-room?"

"That you wouldn't, T.," said Mrs. Tappitt, who was rather carried away by Mrs. Cornbury's eloquence.

"Not in a vestry, because it's joined on to a church," said Tappitt.

"Or would you like a Jew to be mayor in Baslehurst;—a Jew in the chair where you yourself were sitting only three years ago?"

"That wouldn't be seemly, because our mayor is expected to attend in church on Roundabout Sunday." Roundabout Sunday, so called for certain local reasons which it would be long to explain, followed immediately on the day of the mayor's inauguration.

"Would you like to have a Jew partner in your own business?"

Mrs. Butler Cornbury should have said nothing to Mr. Tappitt as to any partner in the brewery, Jew or Christian.

"I don't want any partner, and what's more, I don't mean to have any."

"Mrs. Cornbury is in favour of Luke Rowan; she takes his side," said Mrs. Tappitt, some portion of her courage returning to her as this opportunity opened upon her. Mr. Tappitt turned his head full round and looked upon Mrs. Cornbury with an evil eye. That lady knew that the vote was lost, lost unless she would denounce the man whom Rachel loved; and she determined at once that she would not denounce him. There are many things which such a woman will do to gain such an object. She could smile when Tappitt was offensive; she could smile again when Mrs. Tappitt talked like a kitchenmaid. She could flatter them both, and pretend to talk seriously with them about Jews and her own Church feelings. She could have given up to them Luke Rowan,—if he had stood alone. But she could not give up the girl she had chaperoned, and upon whom, during that chaperoning, her good-will and kindly feelings had fallen. Rachel had pleased her eye, and gratified her sense of feminine nicety. She felt that a word said against Rowan would be a word said also against Rachel; and therefore, throwing her husband over for the nonce, she resolved to sacrifice the vote and stand up for her friend. "Well, yes; I do," said she, meeting Tappitt's eye steadily. She was not going to be looked out of countenance by Mr. Tappitt.

"She thinks he'll come back to marry that young woman at Bragg's End," said Mrs. Tappitt; "but I say that he'll never dare to show his face in Baslehurst again."

"That young woman is making a great fool of herself," said Tappitt, "if she trusts to a swindler like him."

"Perhaps, Mrs. Tappitt," said Mrs. Cornbury, "we needn't mind discussing Miss Ray. It's not good to talk about a young lady in that way, and I'm sure I never said that I thought she was engaged to Mr. Rowan. Had I done so I should have been very wrong, for I know nothing about it. What little I saw of the gentleman I liked;" and as she used the word gentleman she looked Tappitt full in the face; "and for Miss Ray, I've a great regard for her, and think very highly of her. Independently of her acknowledged beauty and pleasant, ladylike manners, she's a very charming girl. About the vote, Mr. Tappitt—; at any rate you'll think of it."

But had he not been defied in his own house? And as for her, the mother of those three finely educated girls, had not every word said in Rachel's favour been a dagger planted in her own maternal bosom? Whose courage would not have risen under such provocation?

Mrs. Cornbury had got up to go, but the indignant, injured Tappitts resolved mutually, though without concert, that she should be answered.

"I'm an honest man, Mrs. Cornbury," said the brewer, "and I like to speak out my mind openly. Mr. Hart is a liberal, and I mean to support my party. Will you tell Mr. Cornbury so with my compliments? It's all nonsense about Jews not being in Parliament. It's not the same as being mayors or churchwardens, or anything like that. I shall vote for Mr. Hart; and, what's more, we shall put him in."

"And Mrs. Cornbury, if you have so much regard for Miss Rachel, you'd better advise her to think no more of that young man. He's no good; he's not indeed. If you ask, you'll find he's in debt everywhere."

"Swindler!" said Tappitt.

"I don't suppose it can be very bad with Miss Rachel yet, for she only saw him about three times,—though she was so intimate with him at our party."

Mrs. Butler Cornbury curtseyed and smiled, and got herself out of the room. Mrs. Tappitt, as soon as she remembered herself, rang the bell, and Mr. Tappitt, following her down to the hall door, went through the pretence of putting her into her carriage.

"She's a nasty meddlesome woman," said Tappitt, as soon as he got back to his wife.

"And how ever she can stand up and say all those things for that girl, passes me!" said Mrs. Tappitt, holding up both her hands. "She was flighty herself, when young; she was, no doubt; and now I suppose she likes others to be the same. If that's what she calls manners, I shouldn't like her to take my girls about."

"And him a gentleman!" said Tappitt. "If those are to be our gentlemen I'd sooner have all the Jews out of Jerusalem. But they'll find out their gentleman; they'll find him out! He'll rob that old mother of his before he's done; you mark my words else." Comforting himself with this hope he took himself back to his counting-house.

Mrs. Cornbury had smiled as she went, and had carried herself through the whole interview without any sign of temper. Even when declaring that she intended to take Rachel's part open-mouthed, she had spoken in a half-drolling way which had divested her words of any tone of offence. But when she got into her carriage, she was in truth very angry. "I don't believe a word of it," she said to herself; "not a word of it." That in which she professed to herself her own disbelief was the general assertion that

Rowan was a swindler, supported by the particular assertion that he had left Baslehurst over head and ears in debt. "I don't believe it." And she resolved that it should be her business to find out whether the accusation were true or false. She knew the ins and outs of Baslehurst life and Baslehurst doings with tolerable accuracy, and was at any rate capable of unravelling such a mystery as that. If the Tappitts in their jealousy were striving to rob Rachel Ray of her husband by spreading false reports, she would encourage Rachel Ray in her love by spreading the truth;—if, as she believed, the truth should speak in Rowan's favour. She would have considerable pleasure in countermining Mr. and Mrs. Tappitt.

As to Mr. Tappitt's vote for the election;—that was gone!

CHAPTER III
DR. HARFORD

The current of events forced upon Rachel a delay of three or four days in answering her letter, or rather forced upon her that delay in learning whether or no she might answer it; and this was felt by her to be a grievous evil. It had been arranged that she should not write until such writing should have received what might almost be called a parochial sanction, and no idea of acting in opposition to that arrangement ever occurred to her; but the more she thought of it the more she was vexed; and the more she thought of it the more she learned to doubt whether or no her mother was placing her in safe tutelage. During these few weeks a great change came upon the girl's character. When first Mrs. Prime had brought home tidings that Miss Pucker had seen her walking and talking with the young man from the brewery, angry as she had been with her sister, and disgusted as she had been with Miss Pucker, she had acknowledged to herself that such talking and walking were very dangerous, if not very improper, and she had half resolved that there should be no more of them. And when Mrs. Prime had seen her standing at the stile, and had brought home that second report, Rachel, knowing what had occurred at that stile, had then felt sure that she was in danger. At that time, though she had thought much of Luke Rowan, she had not thought of him as a man who could possibly be her husband. She had thought of him as having no right to call her Rachel, because he could not possibly become so. There had been great danger;—there had been conduct which she believed to be improper though she could not tell herself that she had been guilty. In her outlook into the world nothing so beautiful had promised itself to her as having such a man to love her as Luke Rowan. Though her mother was not herself ascetic,—liking tea and buttered toast dearly, and liking also little soft laughter with her child,—she had preached ascetisms till Rachel had learned to think that the world was all either ascetic or reprobate. The Dorcas meetings had become distasteful to her because the women were vulgar; but yet she had half believed herself to be wrong in avoiding the work and the vulgarity together. Idle she had never been. Since a needle had come easy to her hand, and the economies of a household had been made intelligible to her, she had earned her bread and assisted in works of charity. She had read no love stories, and been taught to expect no lover. She was not prepared to deny,—did not deny even to herself,—that it was wrong that she should even like to talk to Luke Rowan.

Then came the ball; or, rather, first came the little evening party, which afterwards grew to be a ball. She had been very desirous of going, not for the sake of any pleasure that she promised herself; not for the sake of such pleasure as girls do promise themselves at such gatherings; but because her female pride told her that it was well for her to claim the right of meeting this young man,—well for her to declare that nothing had passed between them which should make her afraid to meet him. That some other hopes had crept in as the evening had come nigh at hand,—hopes of which she had been made aware only by her efforts in repressing them,—may not be denied. She had been accused because of him; and she would show that no such accusation had daunted her. But would he,—would he give occasion for further accusation? She believed he would not; nay, she was sure; at any rate she hoped he would not. She told herself that such was her hope; but had he not noticed her she would have been wretched.

We know now in what manner he had noticed her, and we know also whether she had been wretched. She had certainly fled from him. When she left the brewery-house, inducing Mrs. Cornbury to bring her away, she did so in order that she might escape from him. But she ran from him as one runs from some great joy in order that the mind may revel over it in peace. Then, little as she knew it, her love had been given. Her heart was his. She had placed him upon her pinnacle, and was prepared to worship him. She was ready to dress herself in his eyes, to believe that to be good which he thought good, and to repudiate that which he repudiated. When she bowed her head over his breast a day or two afterwards, she could have spoken to him with the full words of passionate love had not maiden fear repressed her.

But she had not even bowed her head for him, she had not acknowledged to herself that such love was possible to her, till her mother had consented. That her mother's consent had been wavering, doubtful, expressed without intention of such expression,—so expressed that Mrs. Ray hardly knew that she had expressed it,—was not understood by Rachel. Her mother had consented, and, that consent having been given, Rachel was not now disposed to allow of any steps backwards. She seemed to have learned her rights, or to have assumed that she had rights. Hitherto her obedience to her mother had been pure and simple, although, from the greater force of her character, she had in many things been her mother's leader. But now, though she was ill inclined to rebel, though in this matter of the letter she had obeyed, she was beginning to feel that obedience might become a hardship. She did not say to herself, "They have let me love him, and now they must not put out their hands to hold back my love;" but the current of her feelings ran as though such unspoken words had passed across her mind. She had her rights; and though she did not presume that she could insist on them in opposition to her mother or her mother's advisers, she knew that she would be wronged if those rights were withheld from her. The chief of those rights was the possession of her lover. If he was taken from her she would be as one imprisoned unjustly,—as one robbed by those who should have been his friends,—as one injured, wounded, stricken in the dark, and treacherously mutilated by hands that should have protected him. During these days she was silent, and sat with that look upon her brow which her mother feared.

"I could not make Mr. Comfort come any sooner, Rachel," said Mrs. Ray.

"No, mamma."

"I can see how impatient you are."

"I don't know that I'm impatient. I'm sure that I haven't said anything."

"If you said anything I shouldn't mind it so much; but I can't bear to see you with that unhappy look. I'm sure I only wish to do what's best. You can't think it right that you should be writing letters to a gentleman without being sure that it is proper."

"Oh, mamma, don't talk about it!"

"You don't like me to ask your sister; and I'm sure it's natural I should want to ask somebody. He's nearly seventy years old, and he has known you ever since you were born. And then he's a clergyman, and therefore he'll be sure to know what's right. Not that I should have liked to have said a word about it to Mr. Prong, because there's a difference when they come from one doesn't know where."

"Pray, mamma, don't. I haven't made any objection to Mr. Comfort. It isn't nice to be talked over in that way by anybody, that's all."

"But what was I to do? I'm sure I liked the young man very much. I never knew a young man who took his tea so pleasant. And as for his manners and his way of talking, I had it in my heart to fall in love with him myself. I had indeed. As far as that goes, he's just the young man that I could make a son of."

"Dear mamma! my own dearest mamma!" and Rachel, jumping up, threw herself upon her mother's neck. "Stop there. You shan't say another word."

"I'm sure I didn't mean to say anything unpleasant."

"No, you did not; and I won't be impatient."

"Only I can't bear that look. And you know what his mother said,—and Mrs. Tappitt. Not that I care about Mrs. Tappitt; only a person's mother is his mother, and he shouldn't have called her a goose."

It must be acknowledged that Rachel's position was not comfortable; and it certainly would not have been improved had she known how many people in Baslehurst were talking about her and Rowan. That Rowan was gone everybody knew; that he had made love to Rachel everybody said; that he never meant to come back any more most professed to believe. Tappitt's tongue was loud in proclaiming his iniquities; and her follies and injuries Mrs. Tappitt whispered into the ears of all her female acquaintances.

"I'm sorry for her," Miss Harford said, mildly. Mrs. Tappitt was calling at the rectory, and had made her way in. Mr. Tappitt was an upholder of the old rector, and there was a fellow-townsman's friendship between them.

"Oh yes;—very sorry for her," said Mrs. Tappitt.

"Very sorry indeed," said Augusta, who was with her mother.

"She always seemed to me a pretty, quiet, well-behaved girl," said Miss Harford.

"Still waters run deepest, you know, Miss Harford," said Mrs. Tappitt. "I should never have imagined it of her;—never. But she certainly met him half-way."

"But we all thought he was respectable, you know," said Miss Harford.

Miss Harford was thoroughly good-natured; and though she had never gone half-way herself, and had perhaps lost her chance from having been unable to go any part of the way, she was not disposed to condemn a girl for having been willing to be admired by such a one as Luke Rowan.

"Well;—yes; at first we did. He had the name of money, you know, and that goes so far with some girls. We were on our guard,"—and she looked proudly round on Augusta,—"till we should hear what the young man really was. He has thrown off his sheep's clothing now with a vengeance. Mr. Tappitt feels quite ashamed that he should have introduced him to any of the people here; he does indeed."

"That may be her misfortune, and not her fault," said Miss Harford, who in defending Rachel was well enough inclined to give up Luke. Indeed, Baslehurst was beginning to have a settled mind that Luke was a wolf.

"Oh, quite so," said Mrs. Tappitt. "The poor girl has been very unfortunate no doubt."

After that she took her leave of the rectory.

On that evening Mr. Comfort dined with Dr. Harford, as did also Butler Cornbury and his wife, and one or two others. The chances of the election formed, of course, the chief subject of conversation both in the drawing-room and at the dinner-table; but in talking of the election they came to talk of Mr. Tappitt, and in talking of Tappitt they came to talk of Luke Rowan.

It has already been said that Dr. Harford had been rector of Baslehurst for many years at the period to which this story refers. He had nearly completed half a century of work in that capacity, and had certainly been neither an idle nor an inefficient clergyman. But, now in his old age, he was discontented and disgusted by the changes which had come upon him; and though some bodily strength for further service still remained to him, he had no longer any aptitude for useful work. A man cannot change as men change. Individual men are like the separate links of a rotatory chain. The chain goes on with continuous easy motion as though every part of it were capable of adapting itself to a curve, but not the less is each link as stiff and sturdy as any other piece of wrought iron. Dr. Harford had in his time been an active, popular man, —a man possessing even some liberal tendencies in politics, though a country rector of nearly half a century's standing. In his parish he had been more than a clergyman. He had been a magistrate, and a moving man in municipal affairs. He had been a politician, and though now for many years he had supported the Conservative candidate, he had been loudly in favour of the Reform Bill when Baslehurst was a close borough in the possession of a great duke, who held property hard by. But liberal politics had gone on and had left Dr. Harford high and dry on the standing-ground which he had chosen for himself in the early days of his manhood. And then had come that pestilent act of the legislature under which his parish had been divided. Not that the Act of Parliament itself had been violently condemned by the doctor on its becoming law. I doubt whether he had then thought much of it.

But when men calling themselves Commissioners came actually upon him and his, and separated off from him a district of his own town, taking it away altogether from his authority, and giving it over to such inexperienced hands as chance might send thither, —then Dr. Harford became a violent Tory. And my readers must not conceive that this was a question touching his pocket. One might presume that his pocket would be in some degree benefited, seeing that he was saved from the necessity of supplying the spiritual wants of a certain portion of his parish. No shilling was taken from his own income, which, indeed, was by no means excessive. His whole parish gave him barely six hundred a year, out of which he had kept always one, and latterly two curates. It was no question of money in any degree. Sooner than be invaded and mutilated he would have submitted to an order calling upon him to find a third curate,—could any power have given such order. His parish had been invaded and his clerical authority mutilated. He was no longer *totus teres atque rotundus.* The beauty of his life was over, and the contentment of his mind was gone. He knew that it was only left for him to die, spending such days as remained to him in vague prophecies of evil against his devoted country,—a country which had allowed its ancient parochial landmarks to be moved, and its ecclesiastical fastnesses to be invaded!

But perhaps hatred of Mr. Prong was the strongest passion of Dr. Harford's heart at the present moment. He had ever hated the dissenting ministers by whom he was surrounded. In Devonshire dissent has waxed strong for many years, and the pastors of the dissenting flocks have been thorns in the side of the Church of England clergymen. Dr. Harford had undergone his full share of suffering from such thorns. But they had caused him no more than a pleasant irritation in comparison with what he endured from the presence of Mr. Prong in Baslehurst. He would sooner have entertained all the dissenting ministers of the South Hams together than have put his legs under the same mahogany with Mr. Prong. Mr. Prong was to him the evil thing! Anathema! He believed all bad things of Mr. Prong with an absolute faith, but without any ground on which such faith should have been formed. He thought that Mr. Prong drank spirits; that he robbed his parishioners;—Dr. Harford would sooner have lost his tongue than have used such a word with reference to those who attended Mr. Prong's chapel;—that he had left a deserted wife on some parish; that he was probably not in truth ordained. There was nothing which Dr. Harford could not believe of Mr. Prong. Now all this was, to say the least of it, a pity, for it disfigured the close of a useful and conscientious life.

Dr. Harford of course intended to vote for Mr. Cornbury, but he would not join loudly in condemnation of Mr. Tappitt. Tappitt had stood stanchly by him in all parochial contests regarding the new district. Tappitt opposed the Prong faction at all points. Tappitt as churchwarden had been submissive to the doctor. Church of England principles had always been held at the brewery, and Bungall had been ever in favour with Dr. Harford's predecessor.

"He calls himself a Liberal, and always has done," said the doctor. "You can't expect that he should desert his own party."

"But a Jew!" said old Mr. Comfort.

"Well; why not a Jew?" said the doctor. Whereupon Mr. Comfort, and Butler Cornbury, and Dr. Harford's own curate, young Mr. Calclough, and Captain Byng, an old bachelor, who lived in Baslehurst, all stared at him; as Dr. Harford had intended that they should. "Upon my word," said he, "I don't see the use for caring for that kind of thing any longer; I don't indeed. In the way we are going on now, and for the sort of thing we do, I don't see why Jews shouldn't serve us as well in Parliament as Christians. If I am to have my brains knocked out, I'd sooner have it done by a declared enemy than by one who calls himself my friend."

"But our brains are not knocked out yet," said Butler Cornbury.

"I don't know anything about yours, but mine are."

"I don't think the world's coming to an end yet," said the captain.

"Nor do I. I said nothing about the world coming to an end. But if you saw a part of your ship put under the command of a landlubber, who didn't know one side of the vessel from the other, you'd think the world had better come to an end than be carried on in that way."

"It's not the same thing, you know," said the captain. "You couldn't divide a ship."

"Oh, well; you'll see."

"I don't think any Christian should vote for a Jew," said the curate. "A verdict has gone out against them, and what is man that he should reverse it?"

"Are you quite sure that you are reversing it by putting them into Parliament?" said Dr. Harford. "May not that be a carrying on of the curse?"

"There's consolation in that idea for Butler if he loses his election," said Mr. Comfort.

"Parliament isn't what it was," said the doctor. "There's no doubt about that."

"And who is to blame?" said Mr. Comfort, who had never supported the Reform Bill as his neighbour had done.

"I say nothing about blame. It's natural that things should get worse as they grow older."

"Dr. Harford thinks Parliament is worn out," said Butler Cornbury.

"And what if I do think so? Have not other things as great fallen and gone into decay? Did not the Roman senate wear out, as you call it? And as for these Jews, of whom you are speaking, what was the curse upon them but the wearing out of their grace and wisdom? I am inclined to think that we are wearing out; only I wish the garment could have lasted my time without showing so many thin places."

"Now I believe just the contrary," said the captain. "I don't think we have come to our full growth yet."

"Could we lick the French as we did at Trafalgar and Waterloo?" said the doctor.

The captain thought a while before he answered, and then spoke with much solemnity. "Yes," said he, "I think we could. And I hope the time will soon come when we may."

"We shan't do it if we send Jews to Parliament," said Mr. Comfort.

"I must say I think Tappitt wrong," said young Cornbury. "Of course, near as the thing is going, I'm sorry to lose his vote; but I'm not speaking because of that. He has always pretended to hold on to the Church party here, and the Church party has held on to him. His beer is none of the best, and I think he'd have been wise to stick to his old friends."

"I don't see the argument about the beer," said the doctor.

"He shouldn't provoke his neighbours to look at his faults."

"But the Jew's friends would find out that the beer is bad as well as yours."

"The truth is," said Cornbury, "that Tappitt thinks he has a personal grievance against me. He's as cross as a bear with a sore head at the present moment, because this young fellow who was to have been his partner has turned against him. There's some love affair, and my wife has been there and made a mess of it. It's hard upon me, for I don't know that I ever saw the young man in my life."

"I believe that fellow is a scamp," said the doctor.

"I hope not," said Mr. Comfort, thinking of Rachel and her hopes.

"We all hope he isn't, of course," said the doctor. "But we can't prevent men being scamps by hoping. There are other scamps in this town in whom, if my hoping would do any good, a very great change would be made." — Everybody present knew that the doctor alluded especially to Mr. Prong, whose condition, however, if the doctor's hopes could have been carried out, would not have been enviable. — "But I fear this fellow Rowan is a scamp, and I think he has treated Tappitt badly. Tappitt told me all about it only this morning."

"Audi alteram partem," said Mr. Comfort.

"The scamp's party you mean," said the doctor. "I haven't the means of doing that. If in this world we suspend our judgment till we've heard all that can be said on both sides of every question, we should never come to any judgment at all. I hear that he's in debt; I believe he behaved very badly to Tappitt himself, so that Tappitt was forced to use personal violence to defend himself; and he has certainly threatened to open a new brewery here. Now that's bad, as coming from a young man related to the old firm."

"I think he should leave the brewery alone," said Mr. Comfort.

"Of course he should," said the doctor. "And I hear, moreover, that he is playing a wicked game with a girl in your parish."

"I don't know about a wicked game," said the other. "It won't be a wicked game if he marries her."

Then Rachel's chances of matrimonial success were discussed with a degree of vigour which must have been felt by her to be highly complimentary, had she been aware of it. But I grieve to say that public opinion, as expressed in Dr. Harford's dining-room, went against Luke Rowan. Mr. Tappitt was not a great man, either as a citizen or as a brewer: he was not one to whom Baslehurst would even rejoice to raise a monument; but such as he was he had been known for many years. No one in that room loved or felt for him anything like real friendship; but the old familiarity of the place was in his favour, and his form was known of old upon the High Street. He was not a drunkard, he lived becomingly with his wife, he had paid his way, and was a fellow-townsman. What was it to Dr. Harford, or even to Mr. Comfort, that he brewed bad beer? No man was compelled to drink it. Why should not a man employ himself, openly and legitimately, in the brewing of bad beer, if the demand for bad beer were so great as to enable him to live by the occupation? On the other hand, Luke Rowan was personally known to none of them; and they were jealous that a change should come among them with any view of teaching them a lesson or improving their condition. They believed, or thought they believed, that Mr. Tappitt had been ill-treated in his counting-house. It was grievous to them that a man with a wife and three daughters should have been threatened by a young unmarried man, — by a man whose shoulders were laden with no family burden. Whether Rowan's propositions had been in truth good or evil, just or unjust, they had not inquired, and would not probably have ascertained had they done so. But they judged the man and condemned him. Mr. Comfort was brought round to condemn him as thoroughly as did Dr. Harford, — not reflecting, as he did so, how fatal his condemnation might be to the happiness of poor Rachel Ray.

"The fact is, Butler," said the doctor, when Mr. Comfort had left them, and gone to the drawing-room;—"the fact is, your wife has not played her cards at the brewery as well as she usually does play them. She has been taking this young fellow's part; and after that I don't know how she was to expect that Tappitt would stand by you."

"No general can succeed always," said Cornbury, laughing.

"Well; some generals do. But I must confess your wife is generally very successful. Come; we'll go up-stairs; and don't you tell her that I've been finding fault. She's as good as gold, and I can't afford to quarrel with her; but I think she has tripped here."

When the old doctor and Butler Cornbury reached the drawing-room the names of Rowan and Tappitt had not been as yet banished from the conversation; but to them had been added some others. Rachel's name had been again mentioned, as had also that of Rachel's sister.

"Papa, who do you think is going to be married?" said Miss Harford.

"Not you, my dear, is it?" said the doctor.

"Mr. Prong is going to be married to Mrs. Prime," said Miss Harford, showing by the solemnity of her voice that she regarded the subject as one which should by its nature repress any further joke.

Nor was Dr. Harford inclined to joke when he heard such tidings as these. "Mr. Prong!" said he. "Nonsense; who told you?"

"Well, it was Baker told me." Mrs. Baker was the housekeeper at the Baslehurst rectory, and had been so for the last thirty years. "She learned-it at Drabbit's in the High Street, where Mrs. Prime had been living since she left her mother's cottage."

"If that's true, Comfort," said the doctor, "I congratulate you on your parishioner."

"Mrs. Prime is no parishioner of mine," said the vicar of Cawston. "If it's true, I'm very sorry for her mother,—very sorry."

"I don't believe a word of it," said Mrs. Cornbury.

"Poor, wretched, unfortunate woman!" said the doctor. "Her little bit of money is all in her own hands; is it not?"

"I believe it is," said Mr. Comfort.

"Ah, yes; I dare say it's true," said the vicar. "She's been running after him ever since he's been here. I don't doubt it's true. Poor creature!—poor creature! Poor thing!" And the doctor absolutely sighed as he thought of the misery in store for Mr. Prong's future bride. "It's an ill wind that blows nobody any good," he said after a while. "He'll go off, no doubt, when he has got the money in his hand, and we shall be rid of him. Poor thing;—poor thing!"

Before the evening was over Mrs. Cornbury and her father had again discussed the question of Rachel's possible engagement with Luke Rowan. Mr. Comfort had declared his conviction that it would be dangerous to encourage any such hopes; whereas his daughter protested that she would not see Rachel thrown over if she could help it. "Don't condemn him yet, papa," she said.

"I don't condemn him at all, my dear; but I hardly think we shall see him back at Baslehurst. And he shouldn't have gone away without paying his debts, Patty!"

CHAPTER IV
MR. COMFORT CALLS AT THE COTTAGE

Mrs. Ray, in her trouble occasioned by Luke's letter, had walked up to Mr. Comfort's house, but had not found him at home. Therefore she had written to him, in his own study, a few very simple words, telling the matter on which she wanted his advice. Almost any other woman would have half hidden her real meaning under a cloud of ambiguous words; but with her there was no question of hiding anything from her clergyman. "Rachel has had a letter from young Mr. Rowan," she said, "and I have begged her not to answer it till I have shown it to you." So Mr. Comfort sent word down to Bragg's End that he would call at the cottage, and fixed an hour for his coming. This task was to be accomplished by him on the morning after Dr. Harford's dinner; and he had thought much of the coming conference between himself and Rachel's mother while Rowan's character was being discussed at Dr. Harford's house: but on that occasion he had said nothing to any one, not even to his daughter, of the application which had been made to him by Mrs. Ray. At eleven o'clock he presented himself at the cottage door, and, of course, found Mrs. Ray alone. Rachel had taken herself over to Mrs. Sturt, and greatly amazed that kindhearted person by her silence and confusion. "Why, my dear," said Mrs. Sturt, "you hain't got a word to-day to throw at a dog." Rachel acknowledged that she had not; and then Mrs. Sturt allowed her to remain in her silence.

"Oh, Mr. Comfort, this is so good of you!" Mrs. Ray began as soon as her friend was inside the parlour. "When I went up to the parsonage I didn't think of bringing you down here all the way;—I didn't indeed." Mr. Comfort assured her that he thought nothing of the trouble, declared that he owed her a visit, and then asked after Rachel.

"To tell you the truth, then, she's just stept across the green to Mrs. Sturt's, so as to be out of the way. It's a trying time to her, Mr. Comfort,— very; and whatever way it goes, she's a good girl,—a very good girl."

"You needn't tell me that, Mrs. Ray."

"Oh! but I must. There's her sister thinks she's encouraged this young man too freely, but—"

"By-the-by, Mrs. Ray, I've been told that Mrs. Prime is engaged to be married herself."

"Have you, now?"

"Well, yes; I heard it in Baslehurst yesterday;—to Mr. Prong."

"She's kept it so close, Mr. Comfort, I didn't think anybody had heard it."

"It is true, then?"

"I can't say she has accepted him yet. He has offered to her;—there's no doubt about that, Mr. Comfort,—and she hasn't said him no."

"Do let her look sharp after her money," said Mr. Comfort.

"Well, that's just it. She's not a bit inclined to give it up to him, I can tell you."

"I can't say, Mrs. Ray, that the connexion is one that I like very much, in any way. There's no reason at all why your eldest daughter should not marry again, but—"

"What can I do, Mr. Comfort? Of course I know he's not just what he should be,—that is, for a clergyman. When I knew he hadn't come from any of the colleges, I never had any fancy for going to hear him myself. But of course I should never have left your church, Mr. Comfort,—not if anybody had come there. And if I could have had my way with Dorothy, she would never have gone near him,—never. But what could I do, Mr. Comfort? Of course she can go where she likes."

"Mr. Prime was a gentleman and a Christian," said the vicar.

"That he was, Mr. Comfort; and a husband for a young woman to be proud of. But he was soon taken away from her—very soon! and she hasn't thought much of this world since."

"I don't know what she's thinking of now."

"It isn't of herself, Mr. Comfort; not a bit. Dorothy is very stern; but, to give her her due, it's not herself she's thinking of."

"Why does she want to marry him, then?"

"Because he's lonely without some one to do for him."

"Lonely!—and he should be lonely for me, Mrs. Ray."

"And because she says she can work in the vineyard better as a clergyman's wife."

"Pshaw! work in the vineyard, indeed! But it's no business of mine; and, as you say, I suppose you can't help it."

"Indeed I can't. She'd never think of asking me."

"I hope she'll look after her money, that's all. And what's all this about my friend Rachel? I'd a great deal sooner hear that she was going to be married,—if I knew that the man was worthy of her."

Then Mrs. Ray put her hand into her pocket, and taking out Rowan's letter, gave it to the vicar to read. As she did so, she looked into his face with eyes full of the most intense anxiety. She was herself greatly frightened by the magnitude of this marriage question. She feared the enmity of Mrs. Rowan; and she doubted the firmness of Luke. She could not keep herself from reflecting that a young man from London was very dangerous; that he might probably be a wolf; that she could not be safe in trusting her one lamb into such custody. But, nevertheless, she most earnestly hoped that Mr. Comfort's verdict might be in the young man's favour. If he would only say that the young man was not a wolf,—if he would only take upon his own clerical shoulders the responsibility of trusting the young man,— Mrs. Ray would become for the moment one of the happiest women in Devonshire. With what a beaming face,—with what a true joy,—with what smiles through her tears, would she then have welcomed Rachel back from the farm-house! How she would have watched her as she came across the green, beckoning to her eagerly, and telling all her happy tale beforehand by the signs of her joy! But there was to be no such happy tale as that told on this morning. She watched the vicar's face as he read the letter, and soon perceived that the verdict was to be given against the writer of it. I do not know that Mrs. Ray was particularly quick at reading the countenances of men, but, in this instance, she did read the countenance of Mr. Comfort. We, all of us, read more in the faces of those with whom we hold converse, than we are aware of doing. Of the truth, or want of truth in every word spoken to us, we judge, in great part, by the face of the speaker. By the face of every man and woman seen by us, whether they speak or are silent, we form a judgment,—and in nine cases out of ten our judgment is true. It is because our tenth judgment,—that judgment which has been wrong,—comes back upon us always with the effects of its error, that we teach ourselves to say that appearances cannot be trusted. If we did not trust them we should be walking ever in doubt, in darkness, and in ignorance. As Mr. Comfort read the letter, Mrs. Ray knew that it would not be allowed to her to speak words of happiness to Rachel on that day. She knew that the young man was to be set down as dangerous; but she was by no means aware that she was reading the vicar's face with precise accuracy. Mr. Comfort had been slow in his perusal, weighing the words of the letter; and when he had finished it he slowly refolded the paper and put it back into its envelope. "He means what he says," said he, as he gave the letter back to Mrs. Ray.

"Yes; I think he means what he says."

"But we cannot tell how long he may mean it; nor can we tell as yet whether such a connection would be good for Rachel, even if he should remain stedfast in such meaning. If you ask me, Mrs. Ray—"

"I do ask you, Mr. Comfort."

"Then I think we should all of us know more about him, before we allow Rachel to give him encouragement;—I do indeed."

Mrs. Ray could not quite repress in her heart a slight feeling of anger against the vicar. She remembered the words,—so different not only in their meaning, but in the tone in which they were spoken,—in which he had sanctioned Rachel's going to the ball: "Young people get to think of each other," he had then said, speaking with good-humoured, cheery voice, as though such thinking were worthy of all encouragement. He had spoken then of marriage being the happiest condition for both men and women, and had inquired as to Rowan's means. Every word that had then fallen from him had expressed his opinion that Luke Rowan was an eligible lover. But now he was named as though he were undoubtedly a wolf. Why had not Mr. Comfort said then, at that former interview, when no harm had as yet been done, that it would be desirable to know more of the young man before any encouragement was given to him? Mrs. Ray felt that she was injured; but, nevertheless, her trust in her counsellor was not on that account the less.

"I suppose it must be answered," said Mrs. Ray.

"Oh, yes; of course it should be answered."

"And who should write it, Mr. Comfort?"

"Let Rachel write it herself. Let her tell him that she is not prepared to correspond with him as yet, any further that is, you understand, than the writing of that letter."

"And about,—about,—about what he says as to loving her, you know? There has been a sort of promise between them, Mr. Comfort, and no young man could have spoken more honestly than he did."

"And he meant honestly, no doubt; but you see, Mrs. Ray, it is necessary to be so careful in these matters! It is quite evident his mother doesn't wish this marriage."

"And he shouldn't have called her a goose; should he?"

"I don't think much about that."

"Don't you, now?"

"It was all meant in good-humour. But she thinks it a bad marriage for him as regards money, and money considerations always go so far, you know. And then he's away, and you've got no hold upon him."

"That's quite true, Mr. Comfort."

"He has quarrelled with the people here. And upon my word I'm inclined to think he has not behaved very well to Mr. Tappitt."

"Hasn't he, now?"

"I'm afraid not, Mrs. Ray. They were talking about him last night in Baslehurst, and I'm afraid he has behaved badly at the brewery. There were words between him and Mr. Tappitt,—very serious words."

"Yes; I know that. He told Rachel as much as that. I think he said he was going to law with Mr. Tappitt."

"And if so, the chances are that he may never be seen here again. It's ill coming to a place where one is quarrelling with people. And as to the lawsuit, it seems to me, from what I hear, that he would certainly lose it. No doubt he has a considerable property in the brewery; but he wants to be master of everything, and that can't be reasonable, you know. And then, Mrs. Ray, there's worse than that behind."

"Worse than that!" said Mrs. Ray, in whose heart every gleam of comfort was quickly being extinguished by darkening shadows.

"They tell me that he has gone away without paying his debts. If that is so, it shows that his means cannot be very good." Then why had Mr. Comfort taken upon himself expressly to say that they were good at that interview before Mrs. Tappitt's party? That was the thought in the widow's mind at the present moment. Mr. Comfort, however, went on with his caution. "And then, when the happiness of such a girl as Rachel is concerned, it is impossible to be too careful. Where should we all be if we found that we had given her to a scamp?"

"Oh dear, oh dear! I don't think he can be a scamp;—he did take his tea so nicely."

"I don't say he is;—I don't judge him. But then we should be careful. Why didn't he pay his debts before he went away? A young man should always pay his debts."

"Perhaps he's sent it down in a money-order," said Mrs. Ray. "They are so very convenient,—that is if you've got the money."

"If he hasn't I hope he will, for I can assure you I don't want to think badly of him. Maybe he will turn out all right. And you may be sure of this, Mrs. Ray, that if he is really attached to Rachel he won't give her up, because she doesn't throw herself into his arms at his first word. There's nothing becomes a young woman like a little caution, or makes a young man think more of her. If Rachel fancies that she likes him let her hold back a while and find out what sort of stuff he's made of. If I were her I should just tell him that I thought it better to wait a little before I made any positive engagement."

"But, Mr. Comfort, how is she to begin it? You see he calls her Dearest Rachel."

"Let her say Dear Mr. Rowan. There can't be any harm in that."

"She mustn't call him Luke, I suppose."

"I think she'd better not. Young men think so much of those things."

"And she's not to say 'Yours affectionately' at the end?"

"She'll understand all that when she comes to write the letter better than we can tell her. Give her my love; and tell her from me I'm quite sure she's a dear, good girl, and that it must be a great comfort to you to know that you can trust her so thoroughly." Then, having spoken these last words, Mr. Comfort took himself away.

Rachel, sitting in the window of Mrs. Sturt's large front kitchen on the other side of the green, could see Mr. Comfort come forth from the cottage and get into his low four-wheeled carriage, which, with his boy in livery, had been standing at the garden gate during the interview. Mrs. Sturt was away among the milk-pans, scalding cream or preparing butter, and did not watch either Rachel or the visitor at the cottage. But she knew with tolerable accuracy what was going on, and with all her heart wished that her young friend might have luck with her lover. Rachel waited for a minute or two till the little carriage was out of sight, till the sound of the wheels could be no longer heard, and then she prepared to move. She slowly got herself up from her chair as though she were afraid to show herself upon the green, and paused still a few moments longer before she left the kitchen.

"So, thou's off," said Mrs. Sturt, coming in from the back regions of her territory, with the sleeves of her gown tucked up, enveloped in a large roundabout apron which covered almost all her dress. Mrs. Sturt would no more have thought of doing her work in the front kitchen than I should think of doing mine in the drawing-room. "So thou's off home again, my lass," said Mrs. Sturt.

"Yes, Mrs. Sturt. Mr. Comfort has been with mamma,—about business; and as I didn't want to be in the way I just came over to you."

"Thou art welcome, as flowers in May, morning or evening; but thee knowest that, girl. As for Mr. Comfort,—it's cold comfort he is, I always say. It's little I think of what clergymen says, unless it be out of the pulpit or the like of that. What does they know about lads and lasses?"

"He's a very old friend of mamma's."

"Old friends is always best, I'll not deny that. But, look thee here, my girl; my man's an old friend too. He's know'd thee since he lifted thee in his arms to pull the plums off that bough yonder; and he's seen thee these ten years a deal oftener than Mr. Comfort. If they say anything wrong of thy joe there, tell me, and Sturt 'll find out whether it be true or no. Don't let ere a parson in Devonshire rob thee of thy sweetheart. It's passing sweet, when true hearts meet. But it breaks the heart, when true hearts part." With the salutary advice contained in these ancient local lines Mrs. Sturt put her arms round Rachel, and having kissed her, bade her go.

With slow step she made her way across the green, hardly daring to look to the door of the cottage. But there was no figure standing at the door; and let her have looked with all her eyes, there was nothing there to have told her anything. She walked very slowly, thinking as she went of Mrs. Sturt's words—"Don't let ere a parson in Devonshire rob thee of thy sweetheart." Was it not hard upon her that she should be subjected to the misery of such discussion, seeing that she had given no hope, either to her lover or to herself, till she had received full warranty for doing so? She would do what her mother should bid her, let it be what it might; but she would be wronged,—she felt that she would be wronged and injured, grievously injured, if her mother should now bid her think of Rowan as one thinks of those that are gone.

She entered the cottage slowly, and turning into the parlour, found her mother seated there on the old sofa, opposite to the fireplace. She was seated there in stiff composure, waiting the work which she had to do. It was no customary place of hers, and she was a woman who, in the ordinary occupations of her life, never deserted her customary places. She had an old easy chair near the fireplace, and another smaller chair close to the window, and in one of these she might always be found, unless when, on special occasions like the present, some great thing had occurred to throw her out of the grooves of her life.

"Well, mamma?" said Rachel, coming in and standing before her mother. Mrs. Ray, before she spoke, looked up into her child's face, and was afraid. "Well, mamma, what has Mr. Comfort said?"

Was it not hard for Mrs. Ray that at such a moment she should have had no sort of husband on whom to lean? Does the reader remember that in the opening words of this story Mrs. Ray was described as a woman who specially needed some standing-corner, some post, some strong prop to bear her weight,—some marital authority by which she might be guided? Such prop and such guiding she had never needed more sorely than she needed them now. She looked up into Rachel's face before she spoke, and was afraid. "He has been here, my dear," she said, "and has gone away."

"Yes, mamma, I knew that," said Rachel. "I saw his phaeton drive off; that's why I came over from Mrs. Sturt's."

Rachel's voice was hard, and there was no comfort in it. It was so hard that Mrs. Ray felt it to be unkind. No doubt Rachel suffered; but did not she suffer also? Would not she have given blood from her breast, like the maternal pelican, to have secured from that clerical counsellor a verdict that might have been comforting to her child? Would she not have made any sacrifice of self for such a verdict, even though the effecting of it must have been that she herself would have been left alone and deserted in the world? Why, then, should Rachel be stern to her? If misery was to fall on both of them, it was not of her doing.

"I know you will think it's my fault, Rachel; but I cannot help it, even though you should say so. Of course I was obliged to ask some one; and who else was there that would be able to tell me so well as Mr. Comfort? You would not have liked it at all if I had gone to Dorothea; and as for Mr. Prong—"

"Oh! mamma, mamma, don't! I haven't said anything. I haven't complained of Mr. Comfort. What has he said now? You forget that you have not told me."

"No, my dear, I don't forget; I wish I could. He says that Mr. Rowan has behaved badly to Mr. Tappitt, and that he hasn't paid his debts, and that the lawsuit will be sure to go against him, and that he will never show his face in Baslehurst again; and he says, too, that it would be very wrong for you to correspond with him,—very; because a young girl like you must be so careful about such things; and he says he'll be much more likely to respect you if you don't,—don't,—don't just throw yourself into his arms like. Those were his very words; and then he says that if he really cares for you, he'll be sure to come back again, and so you're to answer the letter, and you must call him Dear Mr. Rowan. Don't call him Luke, because young men think so much about those things. And you are to tell him that there isn't to be any engagement, or any letter-writing, or anything of that sort at all. But you can just say something friendly,—about hoping he's quite well, or something of that kind. And then when you come to the end, you had better sign yourself 'Yours truly.' It won't do to say anything about affection, because one never knows how it may turn out. And,—let me see; there was only one thing more. Mr. Comfort says that you are a good girl, and that he is sure you have done nothing wrong,—not even in a word or a thought; and I say so too. You are my own beautiful child; and, Rachel,—I do so wish I could make it all right between you."

Nobody can deny that Mrs. Ray had given, with very fair accuracy, an epitome of Mr. Comfort's words; but they did not leave upon Rachel's mind a very clear idea of what she was expected to do. "Go away in debt!" she said; "who says so?"

"Mr. Comfort told me so just now. But perhaps he'll send the money in a money-order, you know."

"I don't think he would go away in debt. And why should the lawsuit go against him if he's got right on his side? He does not wish to do any harm to Mr. Tappitt."

"I don't know about that, my dear; but at any rate they've quarrelled."

"But why shouldn't that be Mr. Tappitt's fault as much as his? And as for not showing his face in Baslehurst—! Oh, mamma! don't you know him well enough to be sure that he will never be ashamed of showing his face anywhere? He not show his face! Mamma, I don't believe a word of it all,—not a word."

"Mr. Comfort said so; he did indeed." Then Mrs. Sturt's words came back upon Rachel. "Don't let ere a parson in Devonshire rob thee of thy sweetheart." This lover of hers was her only possession,—the only thing of her own winning that she had ever valued. He was her great triumph, the rich upshot of her own prowess,—and now she felt that this parson was indeed robbing her. Had he been then present, she would have risen up and spoken at him, as she had never spoken before. The spirit of rebellion against all the world was strong within her;—against all the world except that one weak woman who now sat before her on the sofa. Her eyes were full of anger, and Mrs. Ray saw that it was so; but still she was minded to obey her mother.

"It's no good talking," said Rachel; "but when they say that he's afraid to show himself in Baslehurst, I don't believe them. Does he look like a man afraid to show himself?"

"Looks are so deceitful, Rachel."

"And as for debts,—people, if they're called away by telegraph in a minute, can't pay all that they owe. There are plenty of people in Baslehurst that owe a deal more than he does, I'm sure. And he's got his share in the brewery, so that nobody need be afraid."

"Mr. Comfort didn't say that you were to quarrel with him altogether."

"Mr. Comfort! What's Mr. Comfort to me, mamma?" This was said in such a tone that Mrs. Ray absolutely started up from her seat.

"But, Rachel, he is my oldest friend. He was your father's friend."

"Why did he not say it before, then? Why—why—why—? Mamma, I can't throw him off now. Didn't I tell him that,—that,—that I would—love him? Didn't you say that it might be so,—you yourself? How am I to show my face, if I go back now? Mamma, I do love him, with all my heart and all my strength, and nothing that anybody can say can make any difference. If he owed ever so much money I should love him the same. If he had killed Mr. Tappitt it wouldn't make any difference."

"Oh, Rachel!"

"No more it would. If Mr. Tappitt began it first, it wasn't his fault."

"But Rachel, my darling,—what can we do? If he has gone away we cannot make him come back again."

"But he wrote almost immediately."

"And you are going to answer it;—are you not?"

"Yes;—but what sort of an answer, mamma? How can I expect that he will ever want to see me again when I have written to him in that way? I won't say anything about hoping that he's very well. If I may not tell him that he's my own, own, own Luke, and that I love him with all my heart, I'll bid him stay away and not trouble himself any further. I wonder what he'll think of me when I write in that way!"

"If he's constant-hearted he'll wait a while and then he'll come back again."

"Why should he come back when I've treated him in that way? What have I got to give him? Mamma, you may write the letter yourself, and put in it what you please."

"Mr. Comfort said that you had better write it."

"Mr. Comfort! I don't know why I'm to do all that Mr. Comfort tells me," and then those other words of Mrs. Sturt's recurred to her, "It's little I think of what a clergyman says unless it be out of a pulpit." After that there was nothing further said for some minutes. Mrs. Ray still sat on the sofa, and as she gazed upon the table which stood in the middle of the room, she wiped her eyes with her handkerchief. Rachel was now seated in a chair with her back almost turned to her mother, and was beating with her impatient fingers on the table. She was very angry,—angry even with her mother; and she was half broken-hearted, truly believing that such a letter as that which she was desired to write would estrange her lover from her for ever. So they sat, and for a few minutes no word was spoken between them.

"Rachel," said Mrs. Ray at last, "if wrong has been done, is it not better that it should be undone?"

"What wrong have I done?" said Rachel, jumping up.

"It is I that have done it,—not you."

"No, mamma; you have done no wrong."

"I should have known more before I let him come here and encouraged you to think of him. It has been my fault. My dear, will you not forgive me?"

"Mamma, there has been no fault. There is nothing to forgive."

"I have made you unhappy, my child," and then Mrs. Ray burst out into open tears.

"No, mamma, I won't be unhappy;—or if I am I will bear it." Then she got up and threw her arms round her mother's neck, and embraced her. "I will write the letter, but I will not write it now. You shall see it before it goes."

CHAPTER V
SHOWING WHAT RACHEL RAY THOUGHT WHEN SHE SAT ON THE STILE, AND HOW SHE WROTE HER LETTER AFTERWARDS

Rachel, as soon as she had made her mother the promise that she would write the letter, left the parlour and went up to her own room. She had many thoughts to adjust in her mind which could not be adjusted satisfactorily otherwise than in solitude, and it was clearly necessary that they should be adjusted before she could write her letter. It must be remembered, not only that she had never before written a letter to a lover, but that she had never before written a letter of importance to any one. She had threatened at one moment that she would leave the writing of it to her mother; but there came upon her a feeling, of which she was hardly conscious, that she herself might probably compose the letter in a strain of higher dignity than her mother would be likely to adopt. That her lover would be gone from her for ever she felt almost assured; but still it would be much to her that, on going, he should so leave her that his respect might remain, though his love would be a thing of the past. In her estimation he was a noble being, to have been loved by whom even for a few days was more honour than she had ever hoped to win. For a few days she had been allowed to think that her great fortune intended him to be her husband. But Fate had interposed, and now she feared that all her joy was at an end. But her joy should be so relinquished that she herself should not be disgraced in the giving of it up. She sat there alone for an hour, and was stronger, when that hour was over, than she had been when she left her mother. Her pride had supported her, and had been sufficient for her support in that first hour of her sorrow. It is ever so with us in our misery. In the first flush of our wretchedness, let the outward signs of our grief be what they may, we promise to ourselves the support of some inner strength which shall suffice to us at any rate as against the eyes of the outer world. But anon, and that inner staff fails us; our pride yields to our tears; our dignity is crushed beneath the load with which we have burdened it, and then with loud wailings we own ourselves to be the wretches which we are. But now Rachel was in the hour of her pride, and as she came down from her room she resolved that her sorrow should be buried in her own bosom. She had known what it was to love,—had known it, perhaps, for one whole week,—and now that knowledge was never to avail her again. Among them all she had been robbed of her sweetheart. She had been bidden to give her heart to this man,—her heart and hand; and now, when she had given all her heart, she was bidden to refuse her hand. She had not ventured to love till her love had been sanctioned. It had been sanctioned, and she had loved; and now that sanction was withdrawn! She knew that she was injured,—deeply, cruelly injured, but she would bear it, showing nothing, and saying nothing. With this resolve she came down from her room, and began to employ herself on her household work.

Mrs. Ray watched her carefully, and Rachel knew that she was watched; but she took no outward notice of it, going on with her work, and saying a soft, gentle word now and again, sometimes to her mother, and sometimes to the little maiden who attended them. "Will you come to dinner, mamma?" she said with a smile, taking her mother by the hand.

"I shouldn't mind if I never sat down to dinner again," said Mrs. Ray.

"Oh, mamma! don't say that; just when you are going to thank God for the good things he gives you."

Then Mrs. Ray, in a low voice, as though rebuked, said the grace, and they sat down together to their meal.

The afternoon went with them very slowly and almost in silence. Neither of them would now speak about Luke Rowan; and to neither of them was it as yet possible to speak about aught else. One word on the subject was said during those hours. "You won't have time for your letter after tea," Mrs. Ray said.

"I shall not write it till to-morrow," Rachel answered; "another day will do no harm now."

At tea Mrs. Ray asked her whether she did not think that a walk would do her good, and offered to accompany her; but Rachel, acceding to the proposition of the walk, declared that she would go alone. "It's very bad of me to say so, isn't it, when you're so good as to offer to go with me?" But Mrs. Ray kissed her; saying, with many words, that she was satisfied that it should be so. "You want to think of things, I know," said the mother. Rachel acknowledged, by a slight motion of her head, that she did want to think of things, and soon after that she started.

"I believe I'll call on Dolly," she said. "It would be bad to quarrel with her; and perhaps now she'll come back here to live with us;—only I forgot about Mr. Prong." It was agreed, however, that she should call on her sister, and ask her to dine at the cottage on the following day.

She walked along the road straight into Baslehurst, and went at once to her sister's lodgings. She had another place to visit before she returned home, but it was a place for which a later hour in the evening would suit her better. Mrs. Prime was at home; and Rachel, on being shown up into the sitting-room,—a room in which every piece of furniture had become known to her during those Dorcas meetings,—found not only her sister sitting there, but also Miss Pucker and Mr. Prong. Rachel had not seen that gentleman since she had learned that he was to become her brother-in-law, and hardly knew in what way to greet him; but it soon became apparent to her that no outward show of regard was expected from her at that moment.

"I think you know my sister, Mr. Prong," said Dorothea. Whereupon Mr. Prong rose from his chair, took Rachel's hand, pressing it between his own, and then sat down again. Rachel, judging from his countenance, thought that some cloud had passed also across the sunlight of his love. She made her little speech, giving her mother's love, and adding her own assurance that she hoped her sister would come out and dine at the cottage.

"I really don't know," said Mrs. Prime. "Such goings about do cut up one's time so much. I shouldn't be here again till—"

"Of course you'd stay for tea with us," said Rachel.

"And lose the whole afternoon!" said Mrs. Prime.

"Oh do!" said Miss Pucker. "You have been working so hard; hasn't she now, Mr. Prong? At this time of the year a sniff of fresh air among the flowers does do a body so much good." And Miss Pucker looked and spoke as though she also would like the sniff of fresh air.

"I'm very well in health, and am thankful for it. I can't say that it's needed in that way," said Mrs. Prime.

"But mamma will be so glad to see you," said Rachel.

"I think you ought to go, Dorothea," said Mr. Prong; and even Rachel could perceive that there was some slight touch of authority in his voice. It was the slightest possible intonation of a command; but, nevertheless, it struck Rachel's ears.

Mrs. Prime merely shook her head and sniffed. It was not for a supply of air that she used her nostrils on this occasion, but that she might indicate some grain of contempt for the authority which Mr. Prong had attempted to exercise. "I think I'd rather not, Rachel, thank you;—not to dinner, that is.

Perhaps I'll walk out in the evening after tea, when the work of the day is over. If I come then, perhaps my friend, Miss Pucker, may come with me."

"And if your esteemed mamma will allow me to pay my respects," said Mr. Prong, "I shall be most happy to accompany the ladies."

It will be acknowledged that Rachel had no alternative left to her. She said that her mother would be happy to see Mr. Prong, and happy to see Miss Pucker also. As to herself, she made no such assertion, being in her present mood too full of her own thoughts to care much for the ordinary courtesies of life.

"I'm very sorry you won't come to dinner, Dolly," she said; but she abstained from any word of asking the others to tea.

"If it had only been Mr. Prong," she said to her mother afterwards, "I should have asked him; for I suppose he'll have to come to the house sooner or later. But I wouldn't tell that horrid, squinting woman that you wanted to see her, for I'm sure you don't."

"But we must give them some cake and a glass of sweet wine," said Mrs. Ray.

"She won't have to take her bonnet off for that as she would for tea, and it isn't so much like making herself at home here. I couldn't bear to have to ask her up to my room."

On leaving the house in the High Street, which she did about eight o'clock, she took her way towards the churchyard,—not passing down Brewery Lane, by Mr. Tappitt's house, but taking the main street which led from the High Street to the church. But at the corner, just as she was about to leave the High Street, she was arrested by a voice that was familiar to her, and, turning round, she saw Mrs. Cornbury seated in a low carriage, and driving a pair of ponies. "How are you, Rachel?" said Mrs. Cornbury, shaking hands with her friend, for Rachel had gone out into the street up to the side of the carriage, when she found that Mrs. Cornbury had stopped. "I'm going by the cottage,—to papa's. I see you are turning the other way; but if you've not much delay, I'll stay for you and take you home."

But Rachel had before her that other visit to make, and she was not minded either to omit it or postpone it. "I should like it so much," said Rachel, "only—"

"Ah! well; I see. You've got other fish to fry. But, Rachel, look here, dear." And Mrs. Cornbury almost whispered into her ear across the side of the pony carriage. "Don't you believe quite all you hear. I'll find out the truth, and you shall know. Good-bye."

"Good-bye, Mrs. Cornbury," said Rachel, pressing her friend's hand as she parted from her. This allusion to her lover had called a blush up over her whole face, so that Mrs. Cornbury well knew that she had been understood. "I'll see to it," she said, driving away her ponies.

See to it! How could she see to it when that letter should have been written? And Rachel was well aware that another day must not pass without the writing of it.

She went down across the churchyard, leaving the path to the brewery on her left, and that leading out under the elm trees to her right, and went on straight to the stile at which she had stood with Luke Rowan, watching the reflection of the setting sun among the clouds. This was the spot which she had determined to visit; and she had come hither hoping that she might again see some form in the heavens which might remind her of that which he had shown her. The stile, at any rate, was the same, and there were the trees beneath which they had stood. There were the rich fields, lying beneath her, over which they two had gazed together at the fading lights of the evening. There was no arm in the clouds now, and the perverse sun was retiring to his rest without any of that royal pageantry and illumination with which the heavens are wont to deck themselves when their king goes to his couch. But Rachel, though she had come thither to look for these things and had not found them, hardly marked their absence. Her mind became so full of him and of his words, that she required no outward signs to refresh her memory. She thought so much of his look on that evening, of the tones of his voice, and of every motion of his body, that she soon forgot to watch the clouds. She sat herself down upon the stile with her face turned away from the fields, telling herself that she would listen for the footsteps of strangers, so that she might move away if any came near her; but she soon forgot also to listen, and sat there thinking of him alone. The words that had been spoken between them on that occasion had been but trifling,—very few and of small moment; but now they seemed to her to have contained all her destiny. It was there that love for him had first come upon her—had come over her with broad outspread wings like an angel; but whether as an angel of darkness or of light, her heart had then been unable to perceive. How well she remembered it all; how he had taken her by the hand, claiming the right of doing so as an ordinary farewell greeting; and how he had held her, looking into her face, till she had been forced to speak some word of rebuke to him! "I did not think you would behave like that," she had said. But yet at that very moment her heart was going from her. The warm friendliness of his touch, the firm, clear brightness of his eye, and the eager tone of his voice, were even then subduing her coy unwillingness to part with her maiden love. She had declared to herself then that she was angry with him; but, since that, she had declared to herself that nothing could have been better, finer, sweeter than all that he had said and done on that evening. It had been his right to hold her, if he intended afterwards to claim her as his own. "I like you so very much," he had said; "why should we not be friends?" She had gone away from him then, fleeing along the path, bewildered, ignorant as to her own feelings, conscious almost of a sin in having listened to him; but still filled with a wondrous delight that any one so good, so beautiful, so powerful as he, should have cared to ask for her friendship in such pressing words. During all her walk home she had been full of fear and wonder and mysterious delight. Then had come the ball, which in itself had hardly been so pleasant to her, because the eyes of many had watched her there. But she thought of the moment when he had first come to her in Mrs. Tappitt's drawing-room, just as she was resolving that he did not intend to notice her further. She thought of those repeated dances which had been so dear to her, but which, in their repetition, had frightened her so grievously. She thought of the supper, during which he had insisted on sitting by her; and of that meeting in the hall, during which he had, as it were, forced her to remain and listen to him,—forced her to stay with him till, in her agony of fear, she had escaped away to her friend and begged that she might be taken home! As she sat by Mrs. Cornbury in the carriage, and afterwards as she had thought of it all while lying in her bed, she had declared to herself that he had been very wrong;—but since that, during those few days of her permitted love, she had sworn to herself as often that he had been very right.

And he had been right. She said so to herself now again, though the words which he had spoken and the things which he had done had brought upon her all this sorrow. He had been right. If he loved her it was only manly and proper in him to tell his love. And for herself,—seeing that she had loved, had it not been proper and womanly in her to declare her love? What had she done; when, at what point, had she gone astray, that she should be brought to such a pass as this? At the beginning, when he had held her hand on the spot where she was now sitting, and again when he had kept her prisoner in Mr. Tappitt's hall, she had been half conscious of some sin, half ashamed of her own conduct; but that undecided fear of sin and shame had been washed out, and everything had been made white as snow, as pure as running water, as bright as sunlight, by the permission to love this man which had been accorded to her. What had she since done that she should be brought to such a pass as that in which she now found herself?

As she thought of this she was bitter against all the world except him;— almost bitter against her own mother. She had said that she would obey in this matter of the letter, and she knew well that she would in truth do as her mother bade her. But, sitting there, on the churchyard stile, she hatched within her mind plans of disobedience,—dreadful plans! She would not submit to this usage. She would go away from Baslehurst without knowledge of any one, and would seek him out in his London home. It would be unmaidenly;—but what cared she now for that;—unless, indeed, he should care? All her virgin modesty and young maiden fears,—was it not for him that she would guard them, for his delight and his pride? And if she were to see him no more, if she were to be forced to bid him go from her, of what avail would it be now to her to cherish and maintain the unsullied brightness of her woman's armour? If he were lost to her, everything was lost. She would go to him, and throwing herself at his feet would swear to him that life without his love was no longer possible for her. If he would then take her as his wife she would strive to bless him with all that the tenderness of a wife could give. If he should refuse her,—then she would go away and die. In such case what to her would be the judgment of any man or any woman? What to her would be her sister's scorn and the malignant virtue of such as Miss Pucker and Mr. Prong? What the upturned hands and amazement of Mr. Comfort? It would have been they who had driven her to this.

But how about her mother when she should have thus thrown herself overboard from the ship and cast herself away from the pilotage which had hitherto been the guide of her conduct? Why—why—why had her mother deserted her in her need? As she thought of her mother she knew that her plan of rebellion was nothing; but why—why had her mother deserted her?

As for him, and these new tidings which had come to the cottage respecting him, she would have cared for them not a jot. Mrs. Cornbury had cautioned her not to believe all that she heard; but she had already declined,—had altogether declined to believe any of it. It was to her, whether believed or disbelieved, matter altogether irrelevant. A wife does not cease to love her husband because he gets into trouble. She does not turn against him because others have quarrelled with him. She does not separate her lot from his because he is in debt! Those are the times when a wife, a true wife, sticks closest to her husband, and strives the hardest to lighten the weight of his cares by the tenderness of her love! And had she not been permitted to place herself in that position with regard to him when she had been permitted to love him? In all her thoughts she recognized the right of her mother to have debarred her from the privilege of loving this man, if such embargo had been placed on her before her love had been declared. She had never, even within her own bosom, assumed to herself the right of such privilege without authority expressed. But her very soul revolted against this withdrawal of the sanction that had been given to her. The spirit within her rebelled, though she knew that she would not carry on that rebellion by word or deed. But she had been injured;—injured almost to death; injured even to death itself as regarded all that life could give her worth her taking! As she thought of this injury that fierce look of which I have spoken came across her brow! She would obey her pastors and masters. Yes; she would obey them. But she could never again be soft and pliable within their hands. Obedience in this matter was a necessity to her. In spite of that wild thought of throwing off her maiden bonds and allowing her female armour to be splashed and sullied in the gutter, she knew that there was that which would hinder her from the execution of such scheme. She was bound by her woman's lot to maintain her womanly purity. Let her suffer as she might there was nothing for her but obedience. She could not go forth as though she were a man, and claim her right to stand or fall by her love. She had been injured in being brought to such plight as this, but she would bear her injury as best might be within her power.

She was still thinking of all this, and still sitting with her eyes turned towards the tower of the church, when she was touched on the back by a light hand. She turned round quickly, startled by the touch,—for she had heard no footstep,—and saw Martha Tappitt and Cherry. It was Cherry who had come close upon her, and it was Cherry's voice that she first heard. "A penny for your thoughts," said Cherry.

"Oh, you have so startled me!" said Rachel.

"Then I suppose your thoughts were worth more than a penny. Perhaps you were thinking of an absent knight." And then Cherry began to sing— "Away, away, away. He loves and he rides away."

Poor Rachel blushed and was unable to speak. "Don't be so foolish," said Martha to her sister. "It's ever so long since we've seen you, Rachel. Why don't you come and walk with us?"

"Yes, indeed,—why don't you?" said Cherry, whose good-nature was quite as conspicuous as her bad taste. She knew now that she had vexed Rachel, and was thoroughly sorry that she had done so. If any other girl had quizzed her about her lover it would not have annoyed her, and she had not understood at first that Rachel Ray might be different from herself. "I declare we have hardly seen you since the night of the party, and we think it very ill-natured in you not to come to us. Do come and walk to-morrow."

"Oh, thank you;—not to-morrow, because my sister is coming out from Baslehurst, to spend the evening with us."

"Well;—on Saturday, then," said Cherry, persistingly.

But Rachel would make no promise to walk with them on any day. She felt that she must henceforth be divided from the Tappitts. Had not he quarrelled with Mr. Tappitt; and could it be fitting that she should keep up any friendship with the family that was hostile to him? She was also aware that Mrs. Tappitt was among those who were desirous of robbing her of her lover. Mrs. Tappitt was her enemy as Mr. Tappitt was his. She asked herself no question as to that duty of forgiving them the injuries they had done her, but she felt that she was divided from them, — from Mr. and Mrs. Tappitt, and also from the girls. And, moreover, in her present strait she wanted no friend. She could not talk to any friend about her lover, and she could not bring herself even to think on any other subject.

"It's late," she said, "and I must go home, as mamma will be expecting me."

Cherry had almost replied that she had not been in so great a hurry once before, when she had stood in the churchyard with another companion; but she thought of Rachel's reproachful face when her last little joke had been uttered, and she refrained.

"She's over head and ears in love," said Cherry to her sister, when Rachel was gone.

"I'm afraid she has been very foolish," said Martha, seriously.

"I don't see that she has been foolish at all. He's a very nice fellow, and as far as I can see he's just as fond of her as she is of him."

"But we know what that means with young men," said Martha, who was sufficiently serious in her way of thinking to hold by that doctrine as to wolves in sheep's clothing in which Mrs. Ray had been educated.

"But young men do marry, — sometimes," said Cherry.

"But not merely for the sake of a pretty face or a good figure. I believe mamma is right in that, and I don't think he'll come back again."

"If he were my lover I'd have him back," said Cherry, stoutly; — and so they went away to the brewery.

Rachel on her way home determined that she would write her letter that night. Her mother was to read it when it was written; that was understood to be the agreement between them; but there would be no reason why she should not be alone when she wrote it. She could word it very differently, she thought, if she sat alone over it in her own bedroom, than she could do immediately under her mother's eye. She could not pause and think and perhaps weep over it, sitting at the parlour table, with her mother in her arm-chair, close by, watching her. It needed that she should write it with tears, with many struggles, with many baffled attempts to find the words that would be wanted,—with her very heart's blood. It must not be tender. No; she was prepared to omit all tenderness. And it must probably be short;—but if so its very shortness would be another difficulty. As she walked along she could not tell herself with what words she would write it; but she thought that the words would perhaps come to her if she waited long enough for them in the solitude of her own chamber.

She reached home by nine o'clock and sat with her mother for an hour, reading out loud some book on which they were then engaged.

"I think I'll go to bed now, mamma," she said.

"You always want to go to bed so soon," said Mrs. Ray. "I think you are getting tired of reading out loud. That will be very sad for me with my eyes."

"No, I'm not, mamma, and I'll go on again for half an hour, if you please; but I thought you liked going to bed at ten."

The watch was consulted, and as it was not quite ten Rachel did go on for another half-hour, and then she went up to her bedroom.

She sat herself down at her open window and looked out for a while upon the heavens. The summer moon was at its full, so that the green before the cottage was as clear before her as in the day, and she could see over into the gloom of Mr. Sturt's farmyard across it. She had once watched Rowan as he came over the turf towards the cottage swinging his stick in his hand, and now she gazed on the spot where the Baslehurst road came in as though she expected that his figure might again appear. She looked and looked, thinking of this, till she would hardly have been surprised had that figure really come forth upon the road. But no figure was to be seen, and after awhile she withdrew from the window and sat herself down at the little table. It was very late when she undressed herself and went to her bed, and later still when her eyes, red with many tears, were closed in sleep;—but the letter had been written and was ready for her mother's inspection. This was the letter as it stood after many struggles in the writing of it,—

> Bragg's End,
> Thursday, 186—

My dear Mr. Rowan,

I am much obliged to you for having written the letter which I received from you the other day, and I should have answered it sooner, only mamma thought it best to see Mr. Comfort first, as he is our clergyman here, and to ask his advice. I hope you will not be annoyed because I showed your letter to mamma, but I could not receive any letter from you without doing so, and I may as well tell you that she will read this before it goes.

And now that I have begun I hardly know how to write what I have to say. Mr. Comfort and mamma have determined that there must be nothing fixed as an engagement between us, and that for the present, at least, I may not correspond with you. This will be my first and last letter. As that will be so, of course I shall not expect you to write any more, and I know that you will be very angry. But if you understood all my feelings I think that perhaps you would not be very, very angry. I know it is true that when you asked me that question, I nodded my head as you say in your letter. If I had sworn the twenty oaths of which you speak they would not, as you say, have bound me tighter. But neither could bind me to anything against mamma's will. I thought that you were very generous to come to me as you did;—oh, so generous! I don't know why you should have looked to such a one as me to be your wife. But I would have done my best to make you happy, had I been able to do as I suppose you then wished me. But you well know that a man is very different from a girl, and of course I must do as mamma wishes.

They say that as the business here about the brewery is so very unsettled they think it probable that you will not have to come back to Baslehurst any more; and that as our acquaintance has been so very short, it is not reasonable to suppose that you will care much about me after a little while. Perhaps it is not reasonable, and after this I shall have no right to be angry with you if you forget me. I don't think you will quite forget me; but I shall never expect or even hope to see you again.

Twice in writing her letter Rachel cut out this latter assertion, but at last, sobbing in despair, she restored the words. What right would she have to hope that he would come to her, after she had taken upon herself to break that promise which had been conveyed to him, when she bent her head over his arm?

I shall not forget you, and I will always be your friend, as you said I should be. Being friends is very different to anything else, and nobody can say that I may not do that.

I will always remember what you showed me in the clouds;
and, indeed, I went there this very evening to see if I could see
another arm. But there was nothing there, and I have taken
that as an omen that you will not come back to Baslehurst.—

"To me," had been the words as she had first written them; but there
was tenderness in those words, and she found it necessary to alter them.

I will now say good-bye to you, for I have told you all that I
have to tell. Mamma desires that I will remember her to you
kindly.

May God bless you and protect you always!

Believe me to be
Your sincere friend,

Rachel Ray.

In the morning she took down the letter in her hand and gave it to her
mother. Mrs. Ray read it very slowly and demurred over it at sundry places.
She especially demurred at that word about the omen, and even declared
that it ought to be expunged. But Rachel was very stern and held her
ground. She had put into the letter, she said, all that she had been bidden to
say. Such a word from herself to one who had been so dear to her must be
allowed to her.

The letter was not altered and was taken away by the postman that
evening.

CHAPTER VI
MRS. RAY GOES TO EXETER,
AND MEETS A FRIEND

Six weeks passed over them at Bragg's End, and nothing was heard of Luke Rowan. Rachel's letter, a copy of which was given in our last chapter, was duly sent away by the postman, but no answer to it came to Bragg's End. It must, however, be acknowledged that it not only required no answer, but that it even refused to be answered. Rachel had told her lover that he was not to correspond with her, and that she certainly would not write to him again. Having so said, she had no right to expect an answer; and she protested over and over again that she did expect none. But still she would watch, as she thought unseen, for the postman's coming; and her heart would sink within her as the man would pass the gate without calling. "He has taken me at my word," she said to herself very bitterly. "I deserve nothing else from him; but—but—but—" In those days she was ever silent and stern. She did all that her mother bade her, but she did little or nothing from love. There were no more banquets, with clotted cream brought over from Mrs. Sturt's. She would speak a word or two now and then to Mrs. Sturt, who understood the whole case perfectly; but such words were spoken on chance occasions, for Rachel now never went over to the farm. Farmer Sturt's assistance had been offered to her; but what could the farmer do for her in such trouble as hers?

During the whole of these six weeks she did her household duties; but gradually she became slower in them and still more slow, and her mother knew that her disappointment was becoming the source of permanent misery. Rachel never said that she was ill; nor, indeed, of any special malady did she show signs: but gradually she became thin and wan, her cheeks assumed a haggard look, and that aspect of the brow which her mother feared had become habitual to her. Mrs. Ray observed her closely in all that she did. She knew well of those watchings for the postman. She was always thinking of her child, and, after a while, longing that Luke Rowan might come back to them, with a heart almost as sore with longing as was that of Rachel herself. But what could she do? She could not bring him back. In all that she had done,—in giving her sanction to this lover, and again in withdrawing it, she had been guided by the advice of her clergyman.

Should she go again to him and beg him to restore that young man to them? Ah! no; great as was her trust in her clergyman she knew that even he could not do that for her.

During all these weeks hardly a word was spoken openly between the mother and daughter about the matter that chiefly occupied the thoughts of them both. Luke Rowan's name was hardly mentioned between them. Once or twice some allusion was made to the subject of the brewery, for it was becoming generally known that the lawyers were already at work on behalf of Rowan's claim; but even on such occasions as these Mrs. Ray found that her speech was stopped by the expression of Rachel's eyes, and by those two lines which on such occasions would mark her forehead. In those days Mrs. Ray became afraid of her younger daughter, —almost more so than she had ever been afraid of the elder one. Rachel, indeed, never spoke as Mrs. Prime would sometimes speak. No word of scolding ever passed her mouth; and in all that she did she was gentle and observant. But there was ever on her countenance that look of reproach which by degrees was becoming almost unendurable. And then her words during the day were so few! She was so anxious to sit alone in her own room! She would still read to her mother for some hours in the evening; but this reading was to her so manifestly a task, difficult and distasteful!

It may be remembered that Mrs. Prime, with her lover, Mr. Prong, and her friend Miss Pucker, had promised to call at Bragg's End on the evening after Rachel's walk into Baslehurst. They did come as they had promised, about half an hour after Rachel's letter to Luke had been carried away by the postman. They had come, and had remained at Bragg's End for an hour, eating cake and drinking currant wine, but not having, on the whole, what our American friends call a good time of it. That visit had been terrible to Mrs. Ray. Rachel had sat there cold, hard, and speechless. Not only had she not asked Miss Pucker to take off her bonnet, but she had absolutely declined to speak to that lady. It was wonderful to her mother that she should thus, in so short a time, have become wilful, masterful, and resolved in following out her own purposes. Not one word on that occasion did she speak to Miss Pucker; and Mrs. Prime, observing this, had grown black and still blacker, till the horror of the visit had become terrible to Mrs. Ray. Miss Pucker had grinned and smiled, and striven gallantly, poor woman, to make the best of it. She had declared how glad she had been to see Miss Rachel on the previous evening, and how well Miss Rachel had looked, and had expressed quite voluminous hopes that Miss Rachel would come to their Dorcas meetings. But to all this Rachel answered not a syllable. Now and then she addressed a word or two to her sister. Now and then she spoke to her mother. When Mr. Prong specially turned himself to her, asking her some question, she would answer him with one or two monosyllables, always calling him Sir; but to Miss Pucker she never once opened her mouth. Mrs. Prime became very angry,—very black and very angry; and the time of the visit was a terrible time to Mrs. Ray.

But this visit is to be noticed in our story chiefly on account of a few words which Mr. Prong found an opportunity of saying to Mrs. Ray respecting his proposed marriage. Mrs. Ray knew that there were difficulties about the money, and was disposed to believe, and perhaps to hope, that the match would be broken off. But on this occasion Mr. Prong was very marked in his way of speaking to Mrs. Ray, as though everything were settled. Mrs. Ray was thoroughly convinced by this that it was so, and her former beliefs and possible hopes were all dispersed. But then Mrs. Ray was easily convinced by any assertion. In thus speaking to his future mother-in-law he had contrived to turn his back round upon the other three ladies, so as to throw them together for the time, and thus make their position the more painful. It must be acknowledged that Rachel was capable of something great, after her determined resistance to Miss Pucker's blandishments under such circumstances as these.

"Mrs. Ray," Mr. Prong had said,—and as he spoke his voice was soft with mingled love and sanctity,—"I cannot let this moment pass without expressing one word of what I feel at the prospect of connecting myself with your amiable family."

"I'm sure I'm much obliged," Mrs. Ray had answered.

"Of course I am aware that Dorothea has mentioned the matter to you."

"Oh yes; she has mentioned it, certainly."

"And therefore I should be remiss, both as regards duty and manners, if I did not take this opportunity of assuring you how much gratification I feel in becoming thus bound up in family affection with you and Miss Rachel. Family ties are sweet bonds of sanctified love; and as I have none of my own,—nearer, that is, than Geelong, the colony of Victoria, where my mother and brother and sisters have located themselves,—I shall feel the more pleasure in taking you and Miss Rachel to my heart."

This was complimentary to Mrs. Ray; but with her peculiar feelings as to the expediency of people having their own belongings, she almost thought that it would have been better for all parties if Mr. Prong had gone to Geelong with the rest of the Prong family: this opinion, however, she did not express. As to taking Mr. Prong to her heart, she felt some doubts of her own capacity for such a performance. It would be natural for her to love a son-in-law. She had loved Mr. Prime very dearly, and trusted him thoroughly. She would have been prepared to love Luke Rowan, had fate been propitious in that quarter. But she could not feel secure as to loving Mr. Prong. Such love, moreover, should come naturally, of its own growth, and not be demanded categorically as a right. It certainly was a pity that Mr. Prong had not made himself happy, with that happiness for which he sighed, in the bosom of his family at Geelong. "I'm sure you're very kind," Mrs. Ray had said.

"And when we are thus united in the bonds of this world," continued Mr. Prong, "I do hope that other bonds, more holy in their nature even than those of family, more needful even than them, may join us together. Dorothea has for some months past been a constant attendant at my church—"

"Oh, I couldn't leave Mr. Comfort; indeed I couldn't," said Mrs. Ray in alarm. "I couldn't go away from my own parish church was it ever so."

"No, no; not altogether, perhaps. I am not sure that it would be desirable. But will it not be sweet, Mrs. Ray, when we are bound together as one family, to pour forth our prayers in holy communion together?"

"I think so much of my own parish church, Mr. Prong," Mrs. Ray replied. After that Mr. Prong did not, on that occasion, press the matter further, and soon turned round his chair so as to relieve the three ladies behind him.

"I think we had better be going, Mr. Prong," said Mrs. Prime, rising from her seat with a display of anger in the very motion of her limbs. "Good-evening, mother: good-evening to you, Rachel. I'm afraid our visit has put you out. Had I guessed as much, we would not have come."

"You know, Dolly, that I am always glad to see you,—only you come to us so seldom," said Rachel. Then with a very cold bow to Miss Pucker, with a very warm pressure of the hand from Mr. Prong, and with a sisterly embrace for Dorothea, that was not cordial as it should have been, she bade them good-bye. It was felt by all of them that the visit had been a failure;—it was felt so, at least, by all the Ray family. Mr. Prong had achieved a certain object in discussing his marriage as a thing settled; and as regarded Miss Pucker, she also had achieved a certain object in eating cake and drinking wine in Mrs. Ray's parlour.

For some weeks after that but little had been seen of Mrs. Prime at the cottage; and nothing had been said of her matrimonial prospects. Rachel did not once go to her sister's lodgings; and, on the few occasions of their meeting, asked no questions as to Mr. Prong. Indeed, as the days and weeks went on, her heart became too heavy to admit of her asking any questions about the love affairs of others. She still went about her work, as I have before said. She was not ill,—not ill so as to demand the care due to an invalid. But she moved about the house slowly, as though her limbs were too heavy for her. She spoke little, unless when her mother addressed her. She would sit for hours on the sofa doing nothing, reading nothing, and looking at nothing. But still, at the postman's morning hours, she would keep her eye upon the road over which he came, and that dull look of despair would come across her face when he passed on without calling at the cottage.

But on a certain morning towards the end of the six weeks the postman did call,—as indeed he had called on other days, though bringing with him no letter from Luke Rowan. Neither now, on this occasion, did he bring a letter from Luke Rowan. The letter was addressed to Mrs. Ray; and, as Rachel well knew from the handwriting, it was from the gentleman who managed her mother's little money matters,—the gentleman who had succeeded to the business left by Mr. Ray when he died. So Rachel took the letter up to her mother and left it, saying that it was from Mr. Goodall.

Mrs. Ray's small income arose partly from certain cottages in Baslehurst, which had been let in lump to a Baslehurst tradesman, and partly from shares in a gas company at Exeter. Now the gas company at Exeter was the better investment of the two, and was considered to be subject to less uncertainty than the cottages. The lease under which the cottages had been let was out, and Mrs. Ray had been advised to sell the property. Building ground near the town was rising in value; and she had been advised by Mr. Goodall to part with her little estate. Both Mrs. Ray and Rachel were aware that this business, to them very important, was imminent; and now had come a letter from Mr. Goodall, saying that Mrs. Ray must go to Exeter to conclude the sale. "We should only bungle matters," Mr. Goodall had said, "if I were to send the deeds down to you; and as it is absolutely necessary that you should understand all about it, I think you had better come up on Tuesday; you can get back to Baslehurst easily on the same day."

"My dear," said Mrs. Ray, coming into the parlour, "I must go to Exeter."

"To-day, mamma?"

"No, not to-day, but on Tuesday. Mr. Goodall says I must understand all about the sale. It is a dreadful trouble."

But, dreadful as the trouble was, it seemed that Mrs. Ray was not made unhappy by the prospect of the little expedition. She fussed and fretted as ladies do on such occasions, but—as is also common with ladies,—the excitement of the journey was, upon the whole, a gratification to her. She asked Rachel to accompany her, and at first pressed her to do so strongly; but such work at the present moment was not in accord with Rachel's mood, and at last she escaped from it under the plea of expense.

"I think it would be foolish, mamma," she said. "Now that Dolly has gone you will be run very close; and when Mr. Goodall first spoke of selling the cottages, he said that perhaps you might be without anything from them for a quarter."

"But he has sold them now, my dear; and there will be the money at once."

"I don't see why you should throw away ten and sixpence, mamma," said Rachel.

And as she spoke in that resolved and masterful tone, her mother, of course, gave up the point. So when the Tuesday morning came, she went with her mother only as far as the station.

"Don't mind meeting me, because I can't be sure about the train," said Mrs. Ray. "But I shall be back to-night, certainly."

"And I'll wait tea for you," said Rachel. Then, when her mother was gone, she walked back to the cottage by herself.

She walked back at once, but took a most devious course. She was determined to avoid the length of the High Street, and she was determined also to avoid Brewery Lane; but she was equally determined to pass through the churchyard. So she walked down from the railway station to the hamlet at the bottom of the hill below the church, and from thence went up by the field-path to the stile. In order to accomplish this she went fully two miles out of her way, and now the sun over her head was very hot. But what was the distance or the heat of the sun to her when her object was to stand for a few moments in that place? Her visit, however, to the spot which was so constantly in her thoughts did her no good. Why had she been so injured? Why had this sacrifice of herself been demanded from her? As she sat for a moment on the stile this was the matter that filled her breast. She had been exalted to the heavens when she first heard her mother speak of Mr. Rowan as an acceptable suitor. She had been filled with joy as though Paradise had been opened to her, when she found herself to be the promised bride of Luke Rowan. Then had come her lover's letter, and the clergyman's counsel, and her own reply; and after that the gates of her Paradise had been closed against her! "I wonder whether it's the same thing to him," she said to herself. "But I suppose not. I don't think it can be the same thing or he would come. Wouldn't I go to him if I were free as he is!" She barely rested in the churchyard, and then walked on between the elms at a quick pace, with a heart sore,—sore almost to breaking. She would never have been brought to this condition had not her mother told her that she might love him! Thence came her vexation of spirit. There was the cruelty. All the world knew that this man had been her lover;—all her world knew it.

Cherry Tappitt had sung her little witless song about it. Mrs. Tappitt had called at the cottage about it. Mr. Comfort had given his advice about it. Mrs. Cornbury had whispered to her about it out of her pony carriage. Mrs. Sturt had counselled her about it. Mr. Prong had thought it very wrong on her part to love the man. Mr. Sturt had thought it very right, and had offered his assistance. All this would have been as nothing had her lover remained to her. Cherry might have sung till her little throat was tired, and Mr. Prong might have expressed his awe with outspread hands, and have looked as though he expected the skies to fall. Had her Paradise not been closed to her, all this talking would have been a thing of course. But such talking,—such wide-spread knowledge of her condition, with the gates of her Paradise closed against her, was very hard to bear! And who had closed the gates? Her own hands had done it. He, her lover, had not deserted her. He had done for her all that truth and earnestness demanded, and perhaps as much as love required. Men were not so soft as girls, she argued within her own breast. Let a man be ever so true it could not be expected that he should stand by his love after he had been treated with such cold indifference as had been shown in her letter! She would have stood by her love, let his letter have been as cold as it might. But then she was a woman, and her love, once encouraged, had become a necessity to her. A man, she said to herself, would be more proud but less stanch. Of course she would hear no more from him. Of course the gates of her Paradise were shut. Such were her thoughts as she walked home, and such the thoughts over which she sat brooding alone throughout the entire day.

At half-past seven in the evening Mrs. Ray came back home, wearily trudging across the green. She was very weary, for she had now walked above two miles from the station. She had also been on her feet half the day, and, which was probably worse than all the rest had she known it, she had travelled nearly eighty miles by railway. She was very tired, and would under ordinary circumstances have been disposed to reckon up her grievances in the evening quite as accurately as Rachel had reckoned hers in the morning. But something had occurred in Exeter, the recollection of which still overcame the sense of weariness which Mrs. Ray felt;—overcame it, or rather overtopped it; so that when Rachel came out to her at the cottage door she did not speak at once of her own weariness, but looked lovingly into her daughter's face,—lovingly and anxiously, and said some little word intended to denote affection.

"You must be very tired," said Rachel, who, with many self-reproaches and much communing within her own bosom, had for the time vanquished her own hard humour.

"Yes, I am tired, my dear; very. I thought the train never would have got to the Baslehurst station. It stopped at all the little stations, and really I think I could have walked as fast." A dozen years had not as yet gone by since the velocity of these trains had been so terrible to Mrs. Ray that she had hardly dared to get into one of them!

"And whom have you seen?" said Rachel.

"Seen!" said Mrs. Ray. "Who told you that I had seen anybody?"

"I suppose you saw Mr. Goodall."

"Oh yes, I saw him of course. I saw him, and the cottages are all sold. We shall have seven pounds ten a year more than before. I'm sure it will be a very great comfort. Seven pounds ten will buy so many things."

"But ten pounds would buy more."

"Of course it would, my dear. And I told Mr. Goodall I wished he could make it ten, as it would make it sound so much more regular like; but he said he couldn't do it because the gas has gone up so much. He could have done it if I had sixty pounds, but of course I hadn't."

"But, mamma, whom did you see except Mr. Goodall? I know you saw somebody, and you must tell me."

"That's nonsense, Rachel. You can't know that I saw anybody." It may, however, be well to explain at once the cause of Mrs. Ray's hesitation, and that this may be done in the proper course, we will go back to her journey to Exeter. All the incidents of her day may be told very shortly; but there was one incident in her day which filled her with so much anxiety, and almost dismay, that it must be narrated.

On arriving at Exeter she got into an omnibus which would have taken her direct to Mr. Goodall's office in the Close; but she was minded to call at a shop in the High Street, and had herself put down at the corner of one of those passages which lead from the High Street to the Close. She got down from the step of the vehicle, very carefully, as is the wont with middle-aged ladies from the country, and turned round to walk directly into the shop; but before her, on the pavement, she saw Luke Rowan. He was standing close to her, so that it was impossible that they should have pretended to miss seeing each other, even had they been so minded. Any such pretence would have been impossible to Mrs. Ray, and would have been altogether contrary to Luke Rowan's nature. He had been coming out of the shop, and had been arrested at once by Mrs. Ray's figure as he saw it emerging from the door of the omnibus.

"How d'you do?" said he, coming forward with outstretched hand, and speaking as though there was nothing between him and Mrs. Ray which required any peculiar word or tone.

"Oh, Mr. Rowan! is this you?" said she. "Dear, dear! I'm sure I didn't expect to see you in Exeter."

"I dare say not, Mrs. Ray; and I didn't expect to see you. But the odd thing is I've come here about the same business as you, though I didn't know anything about it till yesterday."

"What business, Mr. Rowan?"

"I've bought your cottages in Baslehurst."

"No!"

"But I have, and I've paid for them too, and you're going this very minute to Mr. Goodall to sign the deed of sale. Isn't that true? So you see I know all about it."

"Well, that is strange! Isn't it, now?"

"The fact is I must have a bit of land at Baslehurst for building. Tappitt will go on fighting; and as I don't mean to be beaten, I'll have a place of my own there."

"And you'll pull down the cottages?"

"If I don't pull him down first, so as to get the old brewery. I was obliged to buy your bit of ground now, as I might not have been able to get any just when I wanted it. You've sold it a deal too cheap. You tell Mr. Goodall I say so."

"But he says I'm to gain something by selling it."

"Does he? If it is so, I'm very glad of it. I only came down from London yesterday to finish this piece of business, and I'm going back to-day."

During all this time not a word had been said about Rachel. He had not even asked after her in the ordinary way in which men ask after their ordinary acquaintance. He had not looked as though he were in the least embarrassed in speaking to Rachel's mother, and now it seemed as though he were going away, as though all had been said between them that he cared to say. Mrs. Ray at the first moment had dreaded any special word; but now, as he was about to leave her, she felt disappointed that no special word had been spoken. But he was not as yet gone.

"I literally haven't a minute to spare," he said, offering her his hand for a second time; "for I've two or three people to see before I get to the train."

"Good-bye," said Mrs. Ray.

"Good-bye, Mrs. Ray. I don't think I've been very well treated among you. I don't indeed. But I won't say any more about that at present. Is she quite well?"

"Pretty well, thank you," said she, all of a tremble.

"I won't send her any message. As things are at present, no message would be of any service. Good-bye." And so saying he went from her.

Mrs. Ray at that moment had no time for making up her mind as to what she would do or say in consequence of this meeting, — or whether she would do or say anything. She looked forward to all the leisure time of her journey home for thinking of that; so she finished her shopping and hurried on to Mr. Goodall's office without resolving whether or no she would tell Rachel of the encounter. At Mr. Goodall's she remained some little time, dining at that gentleman's house as well as signing the deed, and asking questions about the gas company. He had grateful recollections of kindnesses received from Mr. Ray, and always exercised his hospitality on those rare occasions which brought Mrs. Ray up to Exeter. As they sat at table he asked questions about the young purchaser of the property which somewhat perplexed Mrs. Ray. Yes, she said, she did know him. She had just met him in the street and heard his news. Young Rowan, she told her friend, had been at the cottage more than once, but no mention had been made of his desire to buy these cottages. Was he well spoken of in Baslehurst? Well; — she was so little in Baslehurst that she hardly knew. She had heard that he had quarrelled with Mr. Tappitt, and she believed that many people had said that he was wrong in his quarrel. She knew nothing of his property; but certainly had heard somebody say that he had gone away without paying his debts. It may easily be conceived how miserable and ineffective she would be under this cross-examination, although it was made by Mr. Goodall without any allusion to Rachel.

"At any rate we have got our money," said Mr. Goodall; "and I suppose that's all we care about. But I should say he's rather a harum-scarum sort of fellow. Why he should leave his debts behind him I can't understand, as he seems to have plenty of money."

All this made Mrs. Ray's task the more difficult. During the last two or three weeks she had been wishing that she had not gone to Mr. Comfort, — wishing that she had allowed Rachel to answer Rowan's letter in any terms of warmest love that she might have chosen, — wishing, in fact, that she had permitted the engagement to go on. But now she began again to think that she had been right. If this man were in truth a harum-scarum fellow was it not well that Rachel should be quit of him, — even with any amount of present sorrow? Thinking of this on her way back to Baslehurst she again made up her mind that Rowan was a wolf. But she had not made up her mind as to what she would, or what she would not tell Rachel about the meeting, even when she reached her own door. "I will send her no message," he had said. "As things are at present no message would be of service." What had he meant by this? What purpose on his part did these words indicate? These questions Mrs. Ray had asked herself, but had failed to answer them.

But no resolution on Mrs. Ray's part to keep the meeting secret would have been of avail, even had she made such resolution. The fact would have fallen from her as easily as water falls from a sieve. Rachel would have extracted from her the information, had she been ever so determined not to impart it. As things had turned out she had at once given Rachel to understand that she had met some one in Exeter whom she had not expected to meet.

"But, mamma, whom did you see except Mr. Goodall?" Rachel asked. "I know you saw somebody, and you must tell me."

"That's nonsense, Rachel; you can't know that I saw anybody."

After that there was a pause for some moments, and then Rachel persisted in her inquiry. "But, mamma, I do know that you met somebody." —Then there was another pause. —"Mamma, was it Mr. Rowan?"

Mrs. Ray stood convicted at once. Had she not spoken a word, the form of her countenance when the question was asked would have answered it with sufficient clearness. But she did speak a word. "Well; yes, it was Mr. Rowan. He had come down to Exeter on business."

"And what did he say, mamma?"

"He didn't say anything, —at least, nothing particular. It is he that has bought the cottages, and he had come down from London about that. He told me that he wanted some ground near Baslehurst, because he couldn't get the brewery."

"And what else did he say, mamma?"

"I tell you that he said nothing else."

"He didn't—didn't mention me then?"

Mrs. Ray had been looking away from Rachel during this conversation, — had been purposely looking away from her. But now there was a tone of agony in her child's voice which forced her to glance round. Ah me! She beheld so piteous an expression of woe in Rachel's face that her whole heart was melted within her, and she began to wish instantly that they might have Rowan back again with all his faults.

"Tell me the truth, mamma; I may as well know it."

"Well, my dear, he didn't mention your name, but he did say a word about you."

"What word, mamma?"

"He said he would send no message because it would be no good."

"He said that, did he?"

"Yes, he said that. And so I suppose he meant it would be no good sending anything till he came himself."

"No, mamma; he didn't mean quite that. I understand what he meant. As it is to be so, he was quite right. No message could be of any use. It has been my own doing, and I have no right to blame him. Mamma, if you don't mind, I think I'll go to bed."

"My dear, you're wrong. I'm sure you're wrong. He didn't mean that."

"Didn't he, mamma?" And as she spoke a sad, weary, wobegone smile came over her face,—a smile so sad and piteous that it went to her mother's heart more keenly than would have done any sound of sorrow, any sobs, or wail of grief. "But I think he did mean that, mamma. It's no good doubting or fearing any longer. It's all over now."

"And it has been my fault!"

"No, dearest. It has not been your fault, nor do I think that it has been mine. I think we'd better not talk of faults. Ah dear;—I do wish he had never come here!"

"Perhaps it may be all well yet, Rachel."

"Perhaps it may,—in another world. It will never be well again for me in this. Good-night, mamma. You must never think that I am angry with you."

Then she went up stairs, leaving Mrs. Ray alone with her sorrow.

CHAPTER VII
DOMESTIC POLITICS AT THE BREWERY

In the mean time things were not going on very pleasantly at the brewery, and Mr. Tappitt was making himself unpleasant in the bosom of his family. A lawsuit will sometimes make a man extremely pleasant company to his wife and children. Even a losing lawsuit will sometimes do so, if he be well backed up in his pugnacity by his lawyer, and if the matter of the battle be one in which he can take a delight to fight. "Ah," a man will say, "though I spend a thousand pounds over it, I'll stick to him like a burr. He shan't shake me off." And at such times he is almost sure to be in a good humour, and in a generous mood. Then let his wife ask him for money for a dinner-party, and his daughters for new dresses. He has taught himself for the moment to disregard money, and to think that he can sow five-pound notes broadcast without any inward pangs. But such was by no means the case with Mr. Tappitt. His lawyer Honyman was not backing him up; and as cool reflection came upon him he was afraid of trusting his interests to those other men, Sharpit and Longfite. And Mrs. Tappitt, when cool reflection came on her, had begun to dread the ruin which it seemed possible that terrible young man might inflict upon them. She had learned already, though Mrs. Ray had not, how false had been that report which had declared Luke Rowan to be frivolous, idle, and in debt. To her it was very manifest that Honyman was afraid of the young man; and Honyman, though he might not be as keen as some others, was at any rate honest. Honyman also thought that if the brewery were given up to Rowan that thousand a year which had been promised would be paid regularly; and to this solution of the difficulty Mrs. Tappitt was gradually bending herself to submit as the best which an untoward fate offered to them. Honyman himself had declared to her that Mr. Tappitt, if he were well advised, would admit Rowan in as a partner, on equal terms as regarded power and ultimate possession, but with that lion's share of the immediate concern for himself which Rowan offered. But this she knew that Tappitt would not endure; and she knew, also, that if he were brought to endure it for a while, it would ultimately lead to terrible sorrows. "They would be knocking each other about with the pokers, Mr. Honyman," she had said; "and where would the custom be when that got into the newspapers?" "If I were Mr. Tappitt, I would just let him have his own way," Honyman had replied. "That shows that you don't know Tappitt," had been Mrs. Tappitt's rejoinder. No;— the thousand a year and dignified retirement in a villa had recommended itself to Mrs. Tappitt's mind. She would use all her influence to attain that position,—if only she could bring herself to feel assured that the thousand a year would be forthcoming.

As to Tappitt himself, he was by no means so anxious to prolong the battle as he had been at the time of Rowan's departure. His courage for fighting was not maintained by good backing. Had Honyman clapped him on the shoulder and bade him put ready money in his purse, telling him that all would come out right eventually, and that Rowan would be crushed, he would have gone about Baslehurst boasting loudly, and would have been happy. Then Mrs. T. and the girls would have had a merry time of it; and the Tappitts would have come out of the contest with four or five hundred a year for life instead of the thousand now offered to them, and nobody would have blamed anybody for such a result. But Honyman had not spirit for such backing. In his dull, slow, droning way he had shaken his head and said that things were looking badly. Then Tappitt had cursed and had sworn, and had half resolved to go to Sharpit and Longfite. Sharpit and Longfite would have clapped him on the back readily enough, and have bade him put plenty of money in his purse. But we may suppose that Fate did not intend the ruin of Tappitt, seeing that she did not make him mad enough to seek the counsels of Sharpit and Longfite. Fate only made him very cross and unpleasant in the bosom of his family. Looking out himself for some mode of escape from this terrible enemy that had come upon him, he preferred the raising of the sum of money which would be necessary to buy off Rowan altogether. Rowan had demanded ten thousand pounds, but Tappitt still thought that seven, or, at any rate, eight thousand would do it.

"I don't think he'll take less than ten," said Honyman, "because his share is really worth as much as that."

This was very provoking; and who can wonder that Tappitt was not pleasant company in his own house?

On the day after Mrs. Ray's visit to Exeter, Tappitt, as was now his almost daily practice, made his way into Mr. Honyman's little back room, and sat there with his hat on, discussing his affairs.

"I find that Mr. Rowan has bought those cottages of the widow Ray's," said Honyman.

"Nonsense!" shouted Tappitt, as though such a purchase on Rowan's part was a new injury done to himself.

"Oh, but he has," said Honyman. "There's not a doubt in life about it. If he does mean to build a new brewery, it wouldn't be a bad place. You see it's out of the thoroughfare of the town, and yet, as one may say, within a stone's throw of the High Street."

I will not repeat Mr. Tappitt's exclamation as he listened to these suggestions of his lawyer, but it was of a nature to show that he had not heard the news with indifference.

"You see he's such a fellow that you don't know where to have him," continued Honyman. "It's not only that he don't mind ruining you, but he don't mind ruining himself either."

"I don't believe he's got anything to lose."

"Ah! that's where you're wrong. He has paid ready money for this bit of land to begin with, or Goodall would never have let him have it. Goodall knows what he's about as well as any man."

"And do you mean to tell me that he's going to put up buildings there at once?" And Tappitt's face as he asked the question would have softened the heart of any ordinary lawyer. But Honyman was one whom nothing could harden and nothing soften.

"I don't know what he's going to put up, Mr. Tappitt, and I don't know when. But I know this well enough; that when a man buys little bits of property about a place it shows that he means to do something there."

"If he had twenty thousand pounds, he'd lose it all."

"That's very likely; but the question is, how would you fare in the mean time? If he hadn't this claim upon you, of course you'd let him build what he liked, and only laugh at him." Then Mr. Tappitt uttered another exclamation, and pulling his hat tighter on to his head, walked out of the lawyer's office and returned to the brewery.

They dined at three o'clock at the brewery, and during dinner on this day the father of the family made himself very disagreeable. He scolded the maid-servant till the poor girl didn't know the spoons from the forks. He abused the cook's performances till that valuable old retainer declared that if "master got so rampageous he might suit hisself, the sooner the better; she didn't care how soon; she'd cooked victuals for his betters and would again." He snarled at his daughters till they perked up their faces and came silently to a mutual agreement that they would not condescend to notice him further while he held on in his present mood. And he replied to his wife's questions,—questions intended to be soothing and kindly conjugal,—in such a tone that she determined to have it out with him before she allowed him to go to bed. "She knew her duty," she said to herself, "and she could stand a good deal. But there were some things she couldn't stand and some things that weren't her duty." After dinner Tappitt took himself out at once to his office in the brewery, and then, for the first time, saw the "Baslehurst Gazette and Totnes Chronicle" for that week. The "Baslehurst Gazette and Totnes Chronicle" was an enterprising weekly newspaper, which had been originally intended to convey on Sunday mornings to the inhabitants of South Devonshire the news of the past week, and the paper still bore the dates of successive Sundays. But it had gradually pushed itself out into the light of its own world before its own date, gaining first a night and then a day, till now, at the period of which I am speaking, it was published on the Friday morning.

"You ought just to look at this," a burly old foreman had said, handing him the paper in question, with his broad thumb placed upon a certain column. This foreman had known Bungall, and though he respected Tappitt, he did not fear him. "You should just look at this. Of course it don't amount to nothing; but it's as well to see what folks say." And he handed the paper to his master, almost making a hole in it by screwing his thumb on to the spot he wished to indicate.

Tappitt read the article, and his spirit was very bitter within him. It was a criticism on his own beer written in no friendly tone. "There is no reason," said the article, "why Baslehurst should be flooded with a liquor which no Christian ought to be asked to drink. Baslehurst is as capable of judging good beer from bad as any town in the British empire. Let Mr. Tappitt look to it, or some young rival will spring up beneath his feet and seize from his brow the hop-leaf wreath which Bungall won and wore." This attack was the more cruel because the paper had originally been established by Bungall's money, and had, in old days, been altogether devoted to the Bungall interest. That this paper should turn against him was very hard. But what else had he a right to expect? It was known that he had promised his vote to the Jew candidate, and the paper in question supported the Cornbury interest. A man that lives in a glass house should throw no stones. The brewer who brews bad beer should vote for nobody.

But Tappitt would not regard this attack upon him in its proper political light. Every evil at present falling upon him was supposed to come from his present enemy. "It's that dirty underhand blackguard," he said to the foreman.

"I don't think so, Mr. Tappitt," said the foreman. "I don't think so indeed."

"But I tell you it is," said Tappitt, "and I don't care what you think."

"Just as you please, Mr. Tappitt," said the foreman, who thereupon retired from the office, leaving his master to meditate over the newspaper in solitude.

It was a very bitter time for the poor brewer. He was one of those men whose spirit is not wanting to them while the noise and tumult of contest are around them, but who cannot hold on by their own convictions in the quiet hours. He could storm, and talk loud, and insist on his own way while men stood around him listening and perhaps admiring; but he was cowed when left by himself to think of things which seemed to be adverse. What could he do, if those around him, who had known him all his life as those newspaper people had known him,—what could he do if they turned against him, and talked of bad beer as Rowan had talked? He was not man enough to stand up and face this new enemy unless he were backed by his old friends. Honyman had told him that he would be beaten. How would it fare with him and his family if he were beaten? As he sat in his little office, with his hat low down over his eyes, balancing himself on the hind legs of his chair, he abused Honyman roundly. Had Honyman been possessed of wit, of skill, of professional craft,—had he been the master of any invention, all might have been well. But the attorney was a fool, an ass, a coward. Might it not be that he was a knave? But luckily for Honyman, and luckily also for Mr. Tappitt himself, this abuse did not pass beyond the precincts of Tappitt's own breast. We all know how delightful is the privilege of abusing our nearest friends after this fashion; but we generally satisfy ourselves with that limited audience to which Mr. Tappitt addressed himself on the present occasion.

In the mean time Mrs. Tappitt was sitting up-stairs in the brewery drawing-room with her daughters, and she also was not happy in her mind. She had been snubbed, and almost browbeaten, at dinner time, and she also had had a little conversation in private with Mr. Honyman. She had been snubbed, and, if she did not look well about her, she was going to be ruined. "You mustn't let him go on with this lawsuit," Mr. Honyman had said. "He'll certainly get the worst of it if he does, and then he'll have to pay double." She disliked Rowan quite as keenly as did her husband, but she was fully alive to the folly of spiting Rowan by doing an injury to her own face. She would speak to Tappitt that night very seriously, and in the mean time she turned the Rowan controversy over in her own mind, endeavouring to look at it from all sides. It had never been her custom to make critical remarks on their father's conduct to any of the girls except Martha; but on the present great occasion she waived that rule, and discussed the family affairs in full female family conclave. "I don't know what's come over your papa," she began by saying. "He seems quite beside himself to-day."

"I think he is troubled about Mr. Rowan and this lawsuit," said the sagacious Martha.

"Nasty man! I wish he'd never come near the place," said Augusta.

"I don't know that he's very nasty either," said Cherry. "We all liked him when he was staying here."

"But to be so false to papa!" said Augusta. "I call it swindling, downright swindling."

"One should know and understand all about it before one speaks in that way," said Martha. "I dare say it is very vexatious to papa; but after all perhaps Mr. Rowan may have some right on his side."

"I don't know about right," said Mrs. Tappitt. "I don't think he can have any right to come and set himself up here in opposition, as one may say, to the very ghost of his own uncle. I agree with Augusta, and think it is a very dirty thing to do."

"Quite shameful," said Augusta, indignantly.

"But if he has got the law on his side," continued Mrs. Tappitt, "it's no good your papa trying to go against that. Where should we be if we were to lose everything and be told to pay more money than your papa has got? It wouldn't be very pleasant to be turned out of the house."

"I don't think he'd ever do it," said Cherry.

"I declare, Cherry, I think you are in love with the man," said Augusta.

"If I ain't I know who was," said Cherry.

"As for love," said Mrs. Tappitt, "we all know who is in love with him, — nasty little sly minx! In the whole matter nothing makes me so angry as to think that she should have come here to our dance."

"That was Cherry's doing," said Augusta. This remark Cherry noticed only by a grimace addressed specially to her sister. A battle in Rachel's favour under present circumstances would have been so losing an affair that Cherry had not pluck enough to adventure it on her friend's behalf.

"But the question is, — what are we to do about the lawsuit?" said Mrs. Tappitt. "It is easy to see from your papa's manner that he is very much harassed. He won't admit him as a partner; — that's certain."

"Oh dear! I should hope not," said Augusta.

"That's all very well," said Martha; "but if the young man can prove his right, he must have it. Mamma, do you know what Mr. Honyman says about it?"

"Yes, my dear, I do." Mrs. Tappitt's manner became very solemn, and the girls listened with all their ears. "Yes, my dear, I do. Mr. Honyman thinks your father should give way."

"And take him in as a partner?" said Augusta. "Papa has got that spirit that he couldn't do it."

"It doesn't follow that your papa should take Mr. Rowan in as a partner because he gives up the lawsuit. He might pay him the money that he asks."

"But has he got it?" demanded Martha.

"Besides, it's such a deal; isn't it?" said Augusta.

"Or," continued Mrs. Tappitt, "your papa might accept his offer by retiring with a very handsome income for us all. Your papa has been in business for a great many years, working like a galley-slave. Nobody knows how he has toiled and moiled, except me. It isn't any joke being a brewer,—and having it all on himself as he has had. And if young Rowan ever begins it, I wish him joy of it."

"But would he pay the income?" Martha asked.

"Mr. Honyman says that he would; and if he did not, there would be the property to fall back upon."

"And where should we live?" said Cherry.

"That can't be settled quite yet. It must be somewhere near, so that your papa might keep an eye on the concern, and know that it was going all right. Perhaps Torquay would be the best place."

"Torquay would be delicious," said Cherry.

"And would that man come and live at the brewery?" said Augusta.

"Of course he would, if he pleased," said Martha.

"And bring Rachel Ray with him as his wife?" said Cherry.

"He'll never do that," said Mrs. Tappitt with energy.

"Never; never!" said Augusta,—with more energy.

In this way the large and influential feminine majority of the family at the brewery was brought round to look at one of the propositions made by Rowan without disfavour. It was not that that young man's sins had been in any degree forgiven, but that they all perceived, with female prudence, that it would be injudicious to ruin themselves because they hated him. And then to what lady living in a dingy brick house, close adjoining to the smoke and smells of beer-brewing, would not the idea of a marine villa at Torquay be delicious? None of the family, not even Mrs. Tappitt herself, had ever known what annual profit had accrued to Mr. T. as the reward of his life's work. But they had been required to live in a modest, homely way,—as though that annual profit had not been great. Under the altered circumstances, as now proposed, they would all know that papa had a thousand a year to spend;—and what might not be done at Torquay with a thousand a year? Before Mr. Tappitt came home for the evening,—which he did not do on that day till past ten, having been detained, by business, in the bar of the Dragon Inn,—they had all resolved that the combined ease and dignity of a thousand a year should be accepted.

Mr. Tappitt was still perturbed in spirit when he took himself to the marital chamber. What had been the nature of the business which had detained him at the bar of the Dragon he did not condescend to say, but it seemed to have been of a nature not well adapted to smooth his temper. Mrs. Tappitt perhaps guessed what that business had been; but if so, she said nothing of the subject in direct words. One little remark she did make, which may perhaps have had allusion to that business.

"Bah!" she exclaimed, as Mr. Tappitt came near her; "if you must smoke at all, I wish to goodness you'd smoke good tobacco."

"So I do," said Tappitt, turning round at her sharply. "It's best mixed bird's-eye. As if you could know the difference, indeed!"

"So I do, T. I know the difference very well. It's all poison to me,— absolute poison,—as you're very well aware. But that filthy strong stuff that you've taken to lately, is enough to kill anybody."

"I haven't taken to any filthy strong stuff," said Tappitt.

This was the beginning of that evening's conversation. I am inclined to think that Mrs. Tappitt had made her calculations, and had concluded that she could put forth her coming observations more efficaciously by having her husband in bad humour, than she could, if she succeeded in coaxing him into a good humour. I think that she made the above remarks, not solely because the fumes of tobacco were distasteful to her, but because the possession of a grievance might give her an opportunity of commencing the forthcoming debate with some better amount of justified indignation on her own side. It was not often that she begrudged Tappitt his pipe, or made ill-natured remarks about his gin and water.

"T.," she said, when Tappitt had torn off his coat in some anger at the allusion to "filthy strong stuff,"—"T., what do you mean to do about this lawsuit?"

"I don't mean to do anything."

"That's nonsense, T.; you must do something, you know. What does Mr. Honyman say?"

"Honyman is a fool."

"Nonsense, T.; he's not a fool. Or if he is, why have you let him manage your affairs so long? But I don't believe he's a fool at all. I believe he knows what he's talking about, quite as well as some others, who pretend to be so clever. As to your going to Sharpit and Longfite, it's quite out of the question."

"Who's talking of going to them?"

"You did talk of it."

"No I didn't. You heard me mention their names; but I never said that I should go to them at all. I almost wish I had."

"Now, T., don't talk in that way, or you'll really put me beside myself."

"I don't want to talk of it at all. I only want to go to bed."

"But we must talk of it, T. It's all very well for you to say you don't want to talk of things; but what is to become of me and my girls if everything goes astray at the brewery? You can't expect me to sit by quiet and see you ruined."

"Who talks about my being ruined?"

"Well, I believe all Baslehurst pretty well is talking about it. If a man will go on with a lawsuit when his own lawyer says he oughtn't, what else can come to him but ruin?"

"You don't know anything about it. I wish you'd hold your tongue, and let me go to bed."

"I do know something about it, Mr. Tappitt; and I won't hold my tongue. It's all very well for you to bid me hold my tongue; but am I to sit by and see you ruined, and the girls left without a bit to eat or a thing to wear? Goodness knows I've never thought much about myself. Nobody will ever say that of me. But it has come to this, T.; that something must be settled about Rowan's claim. If he hasn't got justice, he's got law on his side; and he seems to be one of those who don't care much as long as he's got that. If you ask me, T.—"

"But I didn't ask you," said Tappitt.

Tappitt never actually succumbed in these matrimonial encounters, and would always maintain courage for a sharp word, even to the last.

"No, I know you didn't;—and more shame to you, not to consult the wife of your bosom and the mother of your children, when such an affair as this has to be settled. But if you think I'm going to hold my tongue, you're mistaken. I know very well how things are going. You must either let this young man come in as a partner—"

"I'll be — —"

Tappitt would not have disgraced himself by such an exclamation in his wife's bedroom as he then used if his business in the bar of the Dragon had been legitimate.

"Very well, sir. I say nothing about the coarseness of your language on the present occasion, though I might say a great deal if I pleased. But if you don't choose to have him for a partner,—why then you must do something else."

"Of course I must."

"Exactly;—and therefore the only thing is for you to take the offer of a thousand a year that he has made. Now, T., don't begin cursing and swearing again, because you know that can't do any good. Honyman says that he'll pay the income;—and if he don't,—if he gets into arrear with it, then you can come down upon him and turn him out. Think how you'd like that! You've only just to keep a little ready money by you, so that you'll have something for six months or so, if he should get into arrear."

"And I'm to give up everything myself?"

"No, T.; you would not give up anything; quite the other way. You would have every comfort round you that any man can possibly want. You can't go on at it always, toiling and moiling as you're doing now. It's quite dreadful for a man never to have a moment to himself at your time of life, and of course it must tell on any constitution if it's kept up too long. You're not the man you were, T.; and of course you couldn't expect it."

"Oh, bother!"

"That's all very well; but it's my duty to see these things, and to think of them, and to speak of them too. Where should I be, and the girls, if you was hurried into your grave by working too hard?" Mrs. Tappitt's voice, as this terrible suggestion fell from her, was almost poetic, through the depth of its solemnity. "Do you think I don't know what it is that takes you to the Dragon so late at night?"

"I don't go to the Dragon late at night."

"I'm not finding fault, T.; and you needn't answer me so sharp. It's only natural you should want something to sustain you after such slavery as you have to go through. I'm not unreasonable. I know very well what a man is, and what it is he can do, and what he can't. It would be all very well your going on if you had a partner you could trust."

"Nothing on earth shall induce me to carry on with that fellow."

"And therefore you ought to take him at his word and retire. It would be the gentlemanlike thing to do. Of course you'd have the power of going over and seeing that things was straight. And if we was living comfortable at some genteel place, such as Torquay or the like, of course you wouldn't want to be going out to Dragons every evening then. I shouldn't wonder if, in two or three years, you didn't find yourself as strong as ever again."

Tappitt, beneath the clothes, insisted that he was strong; and made some virile remark in answer to that further allusion to the Dragon. He by no means gave way to his wife, or uttered any word of assent; but the lady's scheme had been made known to him; the ice had been broken; and Mrs. Tappitt, when she put out the candle, felt that she had done a good evening's work.

CHAPTER VIII
MRS. RAY'S PENITENCE

Another fortnight went by, and still nothing further was heard at Bragg's End from Luke Rowan. Much was heard of him in Baslehurst. It was soon known by everybody that he had bought the cottages; and there was a widely-spread and well-credited rumour that he was going to commence the necessary buildings for a new brewhouse at once. Nor were these tidings received by Baslehurst with all that horror, — with that loud clamour of indignation, — which Tappitt conceived to be due to them. Baslehurst, I should say, as a whole, received the tidings with applause. Why should not Bungall's nephew carry on a brewery of his own? Especially why should he not, if he were resolved to brew good beer? Very censorious remarks about the Tappitt beer were to be heard in all bar-rooms, and were re-echoed with vehemence in the kitchens of the Baslehurst aristocracy.

"It ain't beer," said Dr. Harford's cook, who had come from the midland counties, and knew what good beer was. "It's a nasty muddle of stuff, not fit for any Christian who has to earn her victuals over a kitchen fire."

It came to pass speedily that Luke Rowan was expected to build a new brewery, and that the event of the first brick was looked for with anxious expectation. And that false report which had spread itself through Baslehurst respecting him and his debts had taken itself off. It had been banished by a contrary report; and there now existed in Baslehurst a very general belief that Rowan was a man of means, — of very considerable means, — a man of substantial capital, whom to have settled in the town would be very beneficial to the community. That false statement as to the bill at Griggs' had been sifted, and the truth made known, — and somewhat to the disgrace of the Tappitt faction. The only article supplied by Griggs to Rowan's order had been the champagne consumed at Tappitt's supper, and for this Rowan had paid ready money within a week of the transaction. It was Mrs. Cornbury who discovered all this, and who employed means for making the truth known in Baslehurst. This truth also became known at last to Mrs. Ray, — but of what avail was it then? She had desired her daughter to treat the young man as a wolf, and as a wolf he had been hounded off from her little sheep-cot. She heard now that he was expected back at Baslehurst; —

that he was a wealthy man; that he was thought well of in the town; that he was going to do great things. With what better possible husband could any young woman have been blessed? And yet she had turned him away from her cottage as though he had been a wolf!

It was from Mrs. Sturt that Mrs. Ray first learned the truth. Mr. Sturt was a tenant on the Cornbury estate, and Mrs. Sturt was of course well known to Mrs. Cornbury. That lady, when she had sifted to the bottom the story of Griggs' bill, and had assured herself that Rowan was by no means minded to surrender his interest in Baslehurst, determined that the truth should be made known to Mrs. Ray. But she was not willing to call on Mrs. Ray herself, nor did she wish to present herself before Rachel at the cottage, unless she could bring with her some more substantial comfort than could be afforded by simple evidence as to Rowan's good character. She therefore took herself to Mrs. Sturt, and discussed the matter with her.

"I suppose she does care about him," said Mrs. Cornbury, sitting in Mrs. Sturt's little parlour that opened out upon the kitchen garden. Mrs. Sturt was also seated, leaning on the corner of the table, with the sleeves of her gown tucked up, ready for work when the Squire's lady should be gone, but very willing to postpone her work as long as the Squire's lady would stay and gossip with her.

"Oh! that she do, Mrs. Butler,—in her heart of hearts. If I know anything of true love, she do love that young man."

"And he did offer to her? There can be no doubt about that, I suppose."

"Not a doubt on earth, Mrs. Butler. She never told me so outright,—nor yet didn't her mother;—but if he didn't, I'll give my head for a cream cheese. Laws love you, Mrs. Butler, I know what's what well enough. I know when a girl's wild and flighty, and thinks of things as she oughtn't;—and I know when she's proper behaved, and gives a young man encouragement only when it becomes her."

"Of course you do, Mrs. Sturt."

"It isn't for me, Mrs. Butler, to say anything against your papa. Nobody can have more respect for their clergyman than Sturt has and I; and before it was all settled like, Sturt never had a word with Mr. Comfort about tithes; but, Mrs. Butler, I think your papa was wrong here. As far as I can learn, it was he that told Mrs. Ray that this young man wasn't all that he should be."

"Papa meant it for the best. There were strange things said about him, you know."

"I never believes one word of what I hears, and never will. People are such liars; bean't they, Mrs. Butler? And I didn't believe a word again him. He's as fine a young man as you'd wish to see in a hundred years, and of course that goes a long way with a young woman. Well, Mrs. Butler, I'll tell Mrs. Ray what you say, but I'm afeard it's too late; I'm afeard it is. He's of a stubborn sort, I think. He's one of them that says, 'If you will not when you may, when you will you shall have nay.'"

Mrs. Cornbury still entertained hope that the stubbornness of the stubborn man might be overcome; but as to that she said nothing to Mrs. Sturt.

Mrs. Sturt, with what friendly tact she possessed, made her communication to Mrs. Ray, but it may be doubted whether more harm than good was not thus done. "And he didn't owe a shilling then?" asked Mrs. Ray.

"Not a shilling," said Mrs. Sturt.

"And he is going to come back to Baslehurst about this brewery business?"

"There's not a doubt in life about that," answered Mrs. Sturt. If these tidings could have come in time they would have been very salutary; but what was Mrs. Ray to do with them now? She felt that she could not honestly withhold them from Rachel; and yet she knew not how to tell them without adding to Rachel's misery. It was very improbable that Rachel should hear anything about Rowan from other lips than her own. It was clear that Mrs. Sturt did not intend to speak to her, and also clear that Mrs. Sturt expected that Mrs. Ray would do so.

Rachel's demeanour at this time was cause of great sorrow to Mrs. Ray. She never smiled. She sought no amusement. She read no books. She spoke but little, and when she did speak her words were hard and cold, and confined almost entirely to household affairs. Her mother knew that she was not ill, because she ate and drank and worked. Even Dorothea must have been satisfied with the amount of needlework which she produced in these days. But though not ill, she was thin and pale, and unlike herself. But perhaps of all the signs which her mother watched so carefully, the signs which tormented her most were those ever-present lines on her daughter's forehead,—lines which Mrs. Ray had now learned to read correctly, and which indicated some settled inward purpose, and an inward resolve that that purpose should become the subject of no outward discussion. Rachel had formerly been everything to her mother;—her friend, her minister, her guide, her great comfort;—the subject on which could be lavished all the soft tenderness of her nature, the loving object to whom could be addressed all the little innocent petulances of her life. But now Mrs. Ray did not dare to be either tender with Rachel, or petulant. She hardly dared to speak to her on subjects that were not indifferent. On this matter of Luke Rowan she did not dare to speak to her. Rachel never upbraided her with words,—had never spoken one word of reproach. But every moment of their passing life was an unspoken reproach, so severe and heavy that the poor mother hardly knew how to bear the burden of her fault.

As Mrs. Ray became more afraid of her younger daughter she became less afraid of the elder. This was occasioned partly, no doubt, by the absence of Mrs. Prime from the cottage. When there she only came as a visitor; and no visitor to a house can hold such dominion there as may be held by a domestic tyrant, present at all meals, and claiming an ascendancy in all conversations. But it arose in part also from the overwhelming solicitude which filled Mrs. Ray's heart from morning to night, as she watched poor Rachel in her misery. Her bowels yearned towards her child, and she longed to give her relief with an excessive longing. Had the man been a very wolf indeed,—such were her feelings at present,—I think that she would have welcomed him to the cottage. In ordering his repulse she had done a deed of which she had by no means anticipated the consequences, and now she repented in the sackcloth and ashes of a sorrow-stricken spirit. Ah me! what could she do to relieve that oppressed one! So thoroughly did this desire override all others in her breast, that she would snub Mrs. Prime without dreading or even thinking of the consequences. Her only hopes and her only fears at the present moment had reference to Rachel. Had Rachel proposed to her that they should both start off to London and there search for Luke Rowan, I doubt whether she would have had the heart to decline the journey.

In these days Mrs. Prime came to the cottage regularly twice a week,—on Wednesdays and Saturdays. On Wednesday she came after tea, and on Saturday she drank tea with her mother. On these occasions much was, of course, said as to the prospect of her marriage with Mr. Prong. Nothing was as yet settled, and Rachel had concluded, in her own mind, that there would be no such wedding. As to Mrs. Ray's opinion, she, of course, thought there would be a wedding or that there would not, in accordance with the last words spoken by Mrs. Prime to herself on the occasion of that special conversation.

"She'll never give up her money," Rachel had said, "and he'll never marry her unless she does."

Mrs. Prime at this period acknowledged to her mother that she was not happy.

"I want," said she, "to do what's right. But it's not always easy to find out what is right."

"That's very true," said Mrs. Ray, thinking that there were difficulties in the affairs of other people quite as embarrassing as those of which Mrs. Prime complained.

"He says," continued the younger widow, "that he wants nothing for himself, but that it is not fitting that a married woman should have a separate income."

"I think he's right there," said Mrs. Ray.

"I quite believe what he says about himself," said Mrs. Prime. "It is not that he wants my money for the money's sake, but that he chooses to dictate to me how I shall use it."

"So he ought if he's to be your husband," said Mrs. Ray.

These conversations usually took place in Rachel's absence. When Mrs. Prime came Rachel would remain long enough to say a word to her, and on the Saturdays would pour out the tea for her and would hand to her the bread and butter with the courtesy due to a visitor; but after that she would take herself to her own bedroom, and only come down when Mrs. Prime had prepared herself for going. At last, on one of these evenings, there came a proposition from Mrs. Prime that she should return to the cottage, and live again with her mother and sister. She had not said that she had absolutely rejected Mr. Prong, but she spoke of her return as though it had become expedient because the cause of her going away had been removed. Very little had been said between her and her mother about Rachel's love affair, nor was Mrs. Prime inclined to say much about it now; but so much as that she did say. "No doubt it's all over now about that young man, and therefore, if you like it, I don't see why I shouldn't come back."

"I don't at all know about it's being all over," said Mrs. Ray, in a hurried quick tone, and as she spoke she blushed with emotion.

"But I suppose it is, mother. From all that I can hear he isn't thinking of her; and I don't suppose he ever did much."

"I don't know what he's thinking about, Dorothea; and I ain't sure that there's any good talking about it. Besides, if you're going to have Mr. Prong at last—"

"If I did, mother, it needn't prevent my coming here for a month or two first. It wouldn't be quite yet certainly,—if at all. And I thought that perhaps, if I am going to settle myself in that way, you'd be glad that we should be altogether again for a little while."

"So I should, Dorothea,—of course. I have never wanted to be divided from my children. Your going away was your own doing, not mine. I'm sure it made me so wretched I didn't know what to do at the time. Only other things have come since, that have pretty nearly put all that out of my mind."

"But you can't think I was wrong to go when I felt it to be right."

"I don't know how that may be," said Mrs. Ray. "If you thought it right to go I suppose you were right to go; but perhaps you shouldn't have had such thoughts."

"Well, mother, we won't go back to that."

"No; we won't, if you please."

"This at any rate is certain, that Rachel, in departing from our usual ways of life, has brought great unhappiness upon herself. I'm afraid she is thinking of this young man now more than she ought to do."

"Of course she is thinking of him. Why should she not think of him?"

"Why, mother! Surely it cannot be good that any girl should think of a man who thinks nothing of her!"

Then Mrs. Ray spoke out,—as perhaps she had never spoken before.

"What right have you to say that he thinks nothing of her? Who can tell? He did think of her,—as honestly as any man ever thought of the woman he wished to mate with. He came to her fairly, and asked her to be his wife. What can any man do more by a girl than that? And she didn't say a word to him to encourage him till those she had a right to look to had encouraged him too. So she didn't. And I don't believe any woman ever had a child that behaved better, or truer, or more maidenly than she has done. And I was a fool, and worse than a fool, when I allowed any one to have an evil thought of her for a moment."

"Do you mean me, mother?"

"I don't mean anybody except myself; so I don't." Mrs. Ray as she spoke was weeping bitterly, and rubbing the tears from her red eyes with her apron. "I've behaved like a fool to her,—worse than a fool,—and I've broken her heart. Not think of him! How's a girl not to think of a man day and night when she loves him better than herself? Think of him! She'll think of him till she's in her grave. She'll think of him till she's past all other thinking. I hate such cruelty; and I hate myself for having been cruel. I shall never forgive myself, the longest day I have to live."

"You only did your duty, mother."

"No; I didn't do my duty at all. It can't be a mother's duty to break her child's heart and to be set against her by what anybody else can say. She was ever and always the best child that ever lived; and she came away from him, and strove to banish him from her thoughts, and wouldn't own to herself that she cared for him the least in the world, till he'd come here and spoken out straight, like a man as he is. I tell you what, Dorothea, I'd go to London, on my knees to him, if I could bring him back to her! I would. And if he comes here, I will go to him."

"Oh, mother!"

"I know he loves her. He's not one of your inconstant ones that take up with a girl for a week or so and then forgets her. But she has offended him, and he's stubborn. She has offended him at my bidding, and it's my doing;—and I'd humble myself in the dust to bring him back to her;—so I would. Never tell me of her not thinking of him. I tell you, Dorothea, she'll think of him always not because she has loved him, but because she has been brought to confess her love."

Mrs. Ray was so strong in her mingled passion and grief, that Mrs. Prime made no attempt to rebuke her. The daughter was indeed quelled by her mother's vehemence, and felt that for the present the subject of Rachel's love and Rachel's lover was not a fitting one for the exercise of her own talents as a preacher. The tragedy had progressed beyond the reach of her preaching. Mrs. Ray protested that Rachel had been right throughout, and that she herself had been wrong only when she had opposed Rachel's wishes. Such a view of the matter was altogether at variance with that entertained by Mrs. Prime, who was still of opinion that young people shouldn't be allowed to please themselves, and who feared the approach of any lover who came with lute in hand, and with light, soft, loving, worldly words. Men and women, according to her theory, were right to marry and have children; but she thought that such marriages should be contracted not only in a solemn spirit, but with a certain dinginess of solemnity, with a painstaking absence of mirth, that would divest love of its worldly alloy. Rachel had gone about her business in a different spirit, and it may almost be said that Mrs. Prime rejoiced that she had failed. She did not believe in broken hearts; she did believe in the efficacy of chastisement; and she thought that on the whole the present state of affairs would be beneficial to her sister. Had she been possessed of sufficient power she would now, on this occasion, have preached her sermon again as she had preached it before; but her mother's passion had overcome her, and she was unable to express her convictions.

"I hope that she will be better soon," she said.

"I hope she will," said Mrs. Ray.

At this moment Rachel came down from her own room and joined them in the parlour. She came in with that same look of sad composure on her face, as though she were determined to speak nothing of her thoughts to any one, and sat herself down near to her sister. In doing so, however, she caught a glimpse of her mother's face, and saw that she had been crying,—saw, indeed, that she was still crying at that moment.

"Mamma," she said, "what is the matter;—has anything happened?"

"No, dear, nothing;—nothing has happened."

"But you would not cry for nothing. What is it, Dolly?"

"We have been talking," said Dorothea. "Things in this world are not so pleasant in themselves that they can always be spoken of without tears,—either outward tears or inward. People are too apt to think that there is no true significance in their words when they say that this world is a vale of tears."

"All the same. I don't like to see mamma crying like that."

"Don't mind it, Rachel," said Mrs. Ray. "If you will not regard me I shall be better soon."

"I was saying that I thought I would come back to the cottage," said Mrs. Prime; "that is, if mother likes it."

"But that did not make mamma cry."

"There were other things arose out of my saying so." Then Rachel asked no further questions, but sat silent, waiting till her sister should go.

"Of course we shall be very glad to have you back again if it suits you to come," said Mrs. Ray. "I don't think it at all nice that a family should be divided,—that is, as long as they are the same family." Having received so much encouragement with reference to her proposed return, Mrs. Prime took her departure and walked back to Baslehurst.

For some minutes after they had been so left, neither Mrs. Ray nor Rachel spoke. The mother sat rocking herself in her chair, and the daughter remained motionless in the seat which she had taken when she first came into the room. Their faces were not turned to each other, but Rachel was so placed that she could watch her mother without being observed. Every now and again Mrs. Ray would put her hand up to her eyes to squeeze away the tears, and a low gurgling sound would come from her, as though she were striving without success to repress her sobs. She had thought that she would speak to Rachel when Mrs. Prime was gone,—that she would confess her error in having sent Rowan away, and implore her child to pardon her and to love her once again. It was not, however, that she doubted Rachel's love,—that she feared that Rachel was casting her out from her heart, or that she was learning to hate her. She knew well enough that her child still loved her. It was this,—that her life had become barren to her, cold, and altogether tasteless without those thousand little signs of ever-present affection to which she had been accustomed. If it was to be always thus between them, what would the world be to her for the remainder of her days? She could have borne to part with Rachel, had Rachel married, as in parting with her she would have looked forward to some future return of her girl's caresses; and in such case she would at least have felt that her loss had come from no cessation of the sweet loving nature of their mutual connexion. She would have wept as she gave Rachel over to a husband, but her tears would have been sweet as well as bitter. But there was nothing of sweetness in her tears as she shed them now,—nothing of satisfaction in her sorrow. If she could get Rachel to talk with her freely on the matter, if she could find an opportunity for confessing herself to have been wrong, might it not be that the soft caresses would be restored to her,—caresses that would be soft, though moistened with salt tears? But she feared to speak to her child. She knew that Rachel's face was still hard and stern, and that her voice was not the voice of other days. She knew that her daughter brooded over the injury that had been done to her,—though she knew also that no accusation was made, even in the girl's own bosom, against herself. She thoroughly understood the state of Rachel's mind, but she was unable to find the words that might serve to soften it.

"I suppose we may as well go to bed," she said at last, giving the matter up, at any rate for that evening.

"Mamma, why were you crying when I came into the room?" said Rachel.

"Was I crying, my dear?"

"You are crying still, mamma. Is it I that make you unhappy?"

Mrs. Ray was anxious to declare that the reverse of that was true,—that it was she who had made the other unhappy; but even now she could not find the words in which to say this. "No," she said; "it isn't you. It isn't anybody. I believe it's true what Mr. Comfort has told us so often when he's preaching. It's all vanity and vexation. There isn't anything to make anybody happy. I suppose I cry because I'm foolisher than other people. I don't know that anybody is happy. I'm sure Dorothea is not, and I'm sure you ain't."

"I don't want you to be unhappy about me, mamma."

"Of course you don't. I know that. But how can I help it when I see how things have gone? I tried to do for the best, and I have—" broken my child's heart, Mrs. Ray intended to say; but she failed altogether before she got as far as that, and bursting out into a flood of tears, hid her face in her apron.

Rachel still kept her seat, and her face was still hard and unmoved. Her mother did not see it; she did not dare to look upon it; but she knew that it was so; she knew her daughter would have been with her, close to her, embracing her, throwing her arms round her, had that face relented. But Rachel still kept her chair, and Mrs. Ray sobbed aloud.

"I wish I could be a comfort to you, mamma," Rachel said after another pause, "but I do not know how. I suppose in time we shall get over this, and things will be as they used to be."

"They'll never be to me as they used to be before he came to Baslehurst," said Mrs. Ray, through her tears.

"At any rate that is not his fault," said Rachel, almost angrily. "Whoever may have done wrong, no one has a right to say that he has done wrong."

"I'm sure I never said so. It is I that have done wrong," exclaimed Mrs. Ray. "I know it all now, and I wish I'd never asked anybody but just my own heart. I didn't mean to say anything against him, and I don't think it. I'm sure I liked him as I never liked any young man the first time of seeing him, that night he came out here to tea; and I know that what they said against him was all false. So I do."

"What was all false, mamma?"

"About his going away in debt, and being a ne'er-do-well, and about his going away from Baslehurst and not coming back any more. Everybody has a good word for him now."

"Have they, mamma?" said Rachel. And Mrs. Ray learned in a moment, from the tone of her daughter's voice, that a change had come over her feeling. She asked her little question with something of the softness of her old manner, with something of the longing loving wishfulness which used to make so many of her questions sweet to her mother's ears. "Have they, mamma?"

"Yes they have, and I believe it was those wicked people at the brewery who spread the reports about him. As for owing anybody money, I believe he's got plenty. Of course he has, or how could he have bought our cottages and paid for them all in a minute? And I believe he'll come back and live at Baslehurst; so I do; only—"

"Only what, mamma?"

"If he's not to come back to you I'd rather that he never showed his face here again."

"He won't come to me, mamma. Had he meant it, he would have sent me a message."

"Perhaps he meant that he wouldn't send the message till he came himself," said Mrs. Ray.

But she made the suggestion in a voice so full of conscious doubt that Rachel knew that she did not believe in it herself.

"I don't think he means that, mamma. If he did why should he keep me in doubt? He is very true and very honest, but I think he is very hard. When I wrote to him in that way after accepting the love he had offered me, he was angered, and felt that I was false to him. He is very honest, but I think he must be very hard."

"I can't think that if he loved you he would be so hard as that."

"Men are different from women, I suppose. I feel about him that whatever he might do I should forgive it. But then I feel, also, that he would never do anything for me to forgive."

"I'll never forgive him, never, if he doesn't come back again."

"Don't say that, mamma. You've no right even to be angry with him, because it was we who told him that there was to be no engagement,—after I had promised him."

"I didn't think he'd take you up so at the first word," said Mrs. Ray;— and then there was again silence for a few minutes.

"Mamma," said Rachel.

"Well, Rachel."

Mrs. Ray was still rocking her chair, and had hardly yet repressed that faint gurgling sound of half-controlled sobs.

"I am so glad to hear you say that you—respect him, and don't believe of him what people have said."

"I don't believe a word bad of him, except that he oughtn't to take huff in that way at one word that a girl says to him. He ought to have known that you couldn't write just what letter you liked, as he could."

"We won't say anything more about that. But as long as you don't think him bad—"

"I don't think him bad. I don't think him bad at all. I think him very good. I'd give all I have in the world to bring him back again. So I would."

"Dear mamma!"

And now Rachel moved away from her chair and came up to her mother.

"And I know it's been all my fault. Oh, my child, I am so unhappy! I don't get half an hour's sleep at night thinking of what I have done;—I, that would have given the very blood out of my veins to make you happy."

"No, mamma; it wasn't you."

"Yes, it was. I'd no business going away to other people after I had told him he might come here. You, who had always been so good too!"

"You mustn't say again that you wish he hadn't come here."

"Oh! but I do wish it, because then he would have been nothing to you. I do wish he hadn't ever come, but now I'd do anything to bring him back again. I believe I'll go to him and tell him that it was my doing."

"No, mamma, you won't do that."

"Why should I not? I don't care what people say. Isn't your happiness everything to me?"

"But I shouldn't take him if he came in that way. What! beg him to come and have compassion on me, as if I couldn't live without him! No, mother; that wouldn't do. I do love him. I do love him. I sometimes think I cannot live without his love. I sometimes feel as though stories about broken hearts might be true. But I wouldn't have him in that way. How could he love me afterwards, when I was his wife? But, mamma, we'll be friends again;—shall we not? I've been so unhappy that you should have thought ill of him!"

That night the mother and daughter shared the same bed together, and Mrs. Ray was able to sleep. She would not confess to herself that her sorrow had been lightened, because nothing had been said or done to lessen that of her daughter; but on the morrow Rachel came and hovered round her again, and the bitterness of Mrs. Ray's grief was removed.

CHAPTER IX
THE ELECTION AT BASLEHURST

Towards the end of September the day of the election arrived, and with it arrived Luke Rowan at Baslehurst. The vacancy had been occasioned by the acceptance of the then sitting member of that situation under the crown which is called the stewardship of the manor of Helpholme. In other words an old gentleman who had done his life's work retired and made room for some one more young and active. The old member had kept his seat till the end of the session, just leaving time for the moving for a new writ, and now the election was about to be held, almost at the earliest day possible. It had been thought that a little reflection would induce the Baslehurst people to reject the smiles of the Jew tailor from London, and therefore as little time for reflection was given to them as possible. The wealth, the liberal politics, the generosity, and the successes of Mr. Hart were dinned into their ears by a succession of speeches, and by an overpowering flight of enormous posters; and then the Jewish hero, the tailor himself, came among them, and astonished their minds by the ease and volubility of his speeches. He did not pronounce his words with any of those soft slushy Judaic utterances by which they had been taught to believe he would disgrace himself. His nose was not hookey, with any especial hook, nor was it thicker at the bridge than was becoming. He was a dapper little man, with bright eyes, quick motion, ready tongue, and a very new hat. It seemed that he knew well how to canvass. He had a smile and a good word for all,—enemies as well as friends. The task of abusing the Cornbury party he left to his committee and backers. He spent a great deal of money,—throwing it away in every direction in which he could do so, without laying himself open to the watchful suspicion of the other side. He ate and drank like a Christian, and only laughed aloud when some true defender of the Protestant faith attempted to scare him away out of the streets by carrying a gammon of bacon up on high. Perhaps his strength as a popular candidate was best shown by his drinking a pint of Tappitt's beer in the little parlour behind the bar at the Dragon.

"He beats me there," said Butler Cornbury, when he heard of that feat.

But the action was a wise one. The question as to Tappitt's brewery and Tappitt's beer was running high at Baslehurst, and in no stronger way could Mr. Hart have bound to him the Tappitt faction than by swallowing in public that pint of beer. "Let me have a small glass of brandy at once," said Mr. Hart to his servant, having retired to his room immediately after the performance of the feat. His constitution was good, and I may as well at once declare that before half an hour had passed over his head he was again himself, and at his work.

The question of Tappitt's beer and Tappitt's brewery was running high in Baslehurst, and had gotten itself involved in the mouths of the people of Baslehurst, not only with the loves and sorrows of poor Rachel Ray, but with the affairs of this election. We know how Tappitt had been driven to declare himself a stanch supporter of the Jew. He had become very stanch,—stanch beyond the promising of his own vote,—stanch even to a final sitting on the Jew's committee, and an active canvasser on the Jew's behalf. His wife, whose passions were less strong than his own and her prudence greater, had remonstrated with him on the matter. "You can vote against Cornbury, if you please," she had said, "but do it quietly. Keep your toe in your pump and say nothing. Just as we stand at present about the business of Rowan's, it would almost be better that you shouldn't vote at all." But Tappitt was an angry man, at this moment uncontrollable by the laws of prudence, and he went into these election matters heart and soul, to his wife's great grief. Butler Cornbury, or Mrs. Butler Cornbury,—it was all the same to him which,—had openly taken up Rowan's part in the brewery controversy. A rumour had reached Tappitt that the inmates of Cornbury Grange had loudly expressed a desire for good beer! Under such circumstances it was not possible for him not to rush to the fight. He did rush into the thick of it, and boasted among his friends that the Jew was safe. I think he was right,— right at any rate as regarded his own peace of mind. Nothing gives a man such spirit for a fight, as the act of fighting. During these election days he was almost regardless of Rowan. He was to second the nomination of the Jew, and so keen was he as to the speech that he would make, and as to the success of what he was doing against Mr. Cornbury, that he was able to talk down his wife, and browbeat Honyman in his own office. Honyman was about to vote for Butler Cornbury, was employed in the Cornbury interest, and knew well on which side his bread was buttered. Sharpit and Longfite were local attorneys for the Jew, and in this way Tappitt was thrown into close intercourse with that eminent firm. "Of course we wouldn't interfere," said Sharpit confidently to the brewer. "We never do interfere with the clients of another firm. We never did such a thing yet, and don't mean to begin. We find people drop into us quick enough without that. But in a friendly way, Mr. Tappitt, let me caution you, not to let your fine business be injured by that young sharper."

Mr. Tappitt found this to be very kind,—and very sensible too. He gave no authority to Sharpit on that occasion to act for him; but he thought of it, resolving that he would set his shoulders firmly to that wheel as soon as he had carried through this business of the election.

But even in the matter of the election everything did not go well with Tappitt. He had appertaining to his establishment a certain foreman of the name of Worts, a heavy, respectable, useful man, educated on the establishment by Bungall and bequeathed by Bungall to Tappitt,—a man by no means ambitious of good beer, but very ambitious of profits to the firm, a servant indeed almost invaluable in such a business. But Tappitt had ever found him deficient in this,—that he had a certain objectionable pride in having been Bungall's servant, and that as such he thought himself absolved from the necessity of subserviency to his latter master. Once a day indeed he did touch his cap, but when that was done he seemed to fancy that he was almost equal to Mr. Tappitt upon the premises. He never shook in his shoes if Tappitt were angry, nor affected to hasten his steps if Tappitt were in a hurry, nor would he even laugh at Tappitt's jokes, if,—as was too usual,— such jokes were not mirth-moving in their intrinsic nature. Clearly he was not at all points a good servant, and Tappitt in some hours of his prosperity had ventured to think that the brewery could go on without him. Now, since the day in which Rowan's treachery had first loomed upon Tappitt, he had felt much inclined to fraternize on easier terms with his foreman. Worts when he touched his cap had been received with a smile, and his advice had been asked in a flattering tone,—not demanded as belonging to the establishment by right. Then Tappitt began to talk of Rowan to his man, and to speak evil things of him, as was natural, expecting a reciprocity of malignity from Worts. But Worts on such occasions had been ominously silent. "H—m, I bean't so zure o' that," Worts had once said, thus differing from his master on some fundamental point of Tappitt strategy as opposed to Rowan strategy. "Ain't you?" said Tappitt, showing his teeth. "You'd better go now and look after those men at the carts." Worts had looked after the men at the carts, but he had done so with an idea in his head that perhaps he would not long look after Tappitt's men or Tappitt's carts. He had not himself been ambitious of good beer, but the idea had almost startled him into acquiescence by its brilliancy.

Now Worts had a vote in the borough, and it came to Tappitt's ears that his servant intended to give that vote to Mr. Cornbury. "Worts," said he, a day or two before the election, "of course you intend to vote for Mr. Hart?"

Worts touched his cap, for it was the commencement of the day.

"I don't jest know," said he. "I was thinking of woting for the young squoire. I've know'd him ever since he was born, and I ain't never know'd the Jew gentleman;—never at all."

"Look here, Worts; if you intend to remain in this establishment I shall expect you to support the liberal interest, as I support it myself. The liberal interest has always been supported in Baslehurst by Bungall and Tappitt ever since Bungall and Tappitt have existed."

"The old maister, he wouldn't a woted for ere a Jew in Christendom,— not agin the squoire. The old maister was allays for the Protestant religion."

"Very well, Worts; there can't be two ways of thinking here, that's all; especially not at such a time as this, when there's more reason than ever why those connected with the brewery should all stand shoulder to shoulder. You've had your bread out of this establishment, Worts, for a great many years."

"And I've 'arned it hard;—no man can't say otherwise. The sweat o' my body belongs to the brewery, but I didn't ever sell 'em my wote;—and I don't mean." Saying which words, with an emphasis that was by no means servile, Worts went out from the presence of his master.

"That man's turning against me," said Tappitt to his wife at breakfast time, in almost mute despair.

"What! Worts?" said Mrs. Tappitt.

"Yes;—the ungrateful hound. He's been about the place almost ever since he could speak, for more than forty years. He's had two pound a week for the last ten years;—and now he's turning against me."

"Is he going over to Rowan?"

"I don't know where the d— — he's going. He's going to vote for Butler Cornbury, and that's enough for me."

"Oh, T., I wouldn't mind that; especially not just now. Only think what a help he'll be to that man!"

"I tell you he shall walk out of the brewery the week after this, if he votes for Cornbury. There isn't room for two opinions here, and I won't have it."

For a moment or two Mrs. Tappitt sat mute, almost in despair. Then she took courage and spoke out.

"T.," said she, "it won't do."

"What won't do?"

"All this won't do. We shall be ruined and left without a home. I don't mind myself; I never did; but think of the girls! What would they do if we was turned out of this?"

"Who's to turn you out?"

"I know. I see it. I am beginning to understand. T., that man would not go against you and the brewery if he didn't know which way the wind is blowing. Worts is wide awake,—quite wide; he always was. T., you must take the offer Rowan has made of a regular income and live retired. If you don't do it,—I shall!" And Mrs. Tappitt, as she spoke the audacious words, rose up from her chair, and stood with her arms leaning upon the table.

"What!" said Tappitt, sitting aghast with his mouth open.

"Yes, T.; if you don't think of your family I must. What I'm saying Mr. Honyman has said before; and indeed all Baslehurst is saying the same thing. There's an offer made to you that will put your family on a footing quite genteel,—no gentlefolks in the county more so; and you, too, that are getting past your work!"

"I ain't getting past my work."

"I shouldn't say so, T., if it weren't for your own good,—and if I'm not to know about that, who is? It's all very well going about electioneering; and indeed it's just what gentlefolks is fit for when they're past their regular work; And I'm sure I shan't begrudge it so long as it don't cost anything; but that's not work you know, T."

"Ain't I in the brewery every day for seven or eight hours, and often more?"

"Yes, T., you are; and what's like to come of it if you go on so? What would be my feelings if I saw you brought into the house struck down with apoplepsy and paralepsy because I let you go on in that way when you wasn't fit? No, T.; I know my duty and I mean to do it. You know Dr. Haustus said only last month that you were that bilious—"

"Pshaw! bilious! it's enough to make any man bilious!"

"Or any dog," he would have added, had he thought of it. Thereupon Tappitt rushed away from his wife, back into his little office, and from that soon made his way to the Jew's committee-room at the Dragon, at which he was detained till nearly eleven o'clock at night.

"It's a kind of work in which one has to do as much after dinner as before," he said to his wife when he got back.

"For the matter of that," said she, "I think the after-dinner work is the chief part of it."

On the day of the election Luke Rowan was to be seen standing in the High Street talking to Butler Cornbury the candidate. Rowan was not an elector, for the cottages had not been in his possession long enough to admit of his obtaining from them a qualification to vote; but he was a declared friend of the Cornbury party. Mrs. Butler Cornbury had sent a message to him saying that she hoped to see him soon after the election should be over: on the following day or on the next, and Butler Cornbury himself had come to him in the town. Though absent from Baslehurst Rowan had managed to declare his opinions before that time, and was suspected by many to have written those articles in the "Baslehurst Gazette" which advocated the right of any constituency to send a Jew to Parliament if it pleased, but which proved at the same time that any constituency must be wrong to send any Jew to Parliament, and that the constituency of Baslehurst would in the present instance be specially wrong to send Mr. Hart to Parliament. "We have always advocated," said one of these articles, "the right of absolute freedom of choice for every borough and every county in the land; but we trust that the day is far distant in which the electors of England shall cease to look to their nearest neighbours as their best representatives." There wasn't much in the argument, but it suited the occasion, and added strength to Rowan's own cause in the borough. All the stanch Protestants began to feel a want of good beer. Questions very ill-natured as toward Tappitt were asked in the newspapers. "Who owns The Spotted Dog at Busby-porcorum; and who compels the landlord to buy his liquor at Tappitt's brewery?" There were scores of questions of the same nature, all of which Tappitt attributed, wrongly, to Luke Rowan. Luke had written that article about freedom of election, but he had not condescended to notice the beer at the Spotted Dog.

And there was another quarrel taking place in Baslehurst, on the score of that election, between persons with whom we are connected in this story. Mr. Prong had a vote in the borough, and was disposed to make use of it; and Mrs. Prime, regarding her own position as Mr. Prong's affianced bride, considered herself at liberty to question Mr. Prong as to the use which he proposed to make of that vote. To Mrs. Prime it appeared that anything done in any direction for the benefit of a Jew was a sin not to be forgiven. To Mr. Prong it seemed to be as great a sin not to do anything in his power for the hindrance and vexation of those with whom Dr. Harford and Mr. Comfort were connected by ties of friendship. Mrs. Prime, who, of the two, was the more logical, would not disjoin her personal and her scriptural hatreds. She also hated Dr. Harford; but she hated the Jews more. She was not disposed to support a Jew in Baslehurst because Mr. Comfort, in his doctrines, had fallen away from the purity of his early promise. Her idea was that a just man and a good Christian could not vote for either of the Baslehurst candidates under the present unhappy local circumstances;—but that under no circumstances should a Christian vote for a Jew. All this she said, in a voice not so soft as should be the voice of woman to her betrothed.

"Dorothea," said Mr. Prong very solemnly;—they were sitting at the time in his own little front parlour, as to the due arrangement of the furniture in which Mrs. Prime had already ventured to make some slight alterations which had not been received favourably by Mr. Prong,— "Dorothea, in this matter you must allow me to be the best judge. Voting for Members of Parliament is a thing which ladies naturally are not called upon to understand."

"Ladies can understand as well as gentlemen," said Mrs. Prime, "that a curse has gone out from the Lord against that people; and gentlemen have no more right than ladies to go against the will of the Lord."

It was in vain that Mr. Prong endeavoured to explain to her that the curse attached to the people as a nation, and did not necessarily follow units of that people who had adopted other nationalities.

"Let the units become Christians before they go into Parliament," said Mrs. Prime.

"I wish they would," said Mr. Prong. "I heartily wish they would: and Mr. Hart, if he be returned, shall have my prayers."

But this did not at all suffice for Mrs. Prime, who, perhaps, in the matter of argument had the best of it. She told her betrothed to his face that he was going to commit a great sin, and that he was tempted to this sin by grievous worldly passions. When so informed Mr. Prong closed his eyes, crossed his hands meekly on his breast, and shook his head.

"Not from thee, Dorothea," said he, "not from thee should this have come."

"Who is to speak out to you if I am not?" said she.

But Mr. Prong sat in silence, and with closed eyes again shook his head.

"Perhaps we had better part," said Mrs. Prime, after an interval of five minutes. "Perhaps it will be better for both of us."

Mr. Prong, however, still shook his head in silence; and it was difficult for a lady in Mrs. Prime's position to read accurately the meaning of such shakings under such circumstances. But Mrs. Prime was a woman sufficiently versed in the world's business to be able to resolve that she would have an answer to her question when she required an answer.

"Mr. Prong," she said, "I remarked just now that perhaps we had better part."

"I heard the words," said Mr. Prong,—"I heard the cruel words." But even then he did not open his eyes, or remove his hands from his breast. "I heard the words, and I heard those other words, still more cruel. You had better leave me now that I may humble myself in prayer."

"That's all very well, Mr. Prong, and I'm sure I hope you will; but situated as we are, of course I should choose to have an answer. It seems to me that you dislike that kind of interference which I regard as a wife's best privilege and sweetest duty. If this be so, it will be better for us to part,—as friends of course."

"You have accused me of a great sin," he said; "of a great sin;—of a great sin!"

"And so in my mind it would be."

"Judge not, lest ye be judged, Dorothea; remember that."

"That doesn't mean, Mr. Prong, that we are not to have our opinions, and that we are not to warn those that are near us when we see them walking in the wrong path. I might as well say the same to you, when you—"

"No, Dorothea; it is my bounden duty. It is my work. It is that to which I am appointed as a minister. If you cannot see the difference I have much mistaken your character,—have much mistaken your character."

"Do you mean to say that nobody but a clergyman is to know what's right and what's wrong? That must be nonsense, Mr. Prong. I'm sorry to say anything to grieve you,—" Mr. Prong was now shaking his head again, with his eyes most pertinaciously closed,—"but there are some things which really one can't bear."

But he only shook his head. His inward feelings were too many for him, so that he could not at the present moment bring himself to give a reply to the momentous proposition which his betrothed had made him. Nor, indeed, had he at this moment fixed his mind as to the step which Duty and Wisdom combined would call upon him to take in this matter. The temper of the lady was not certainly all that he had desired. As an admiring member of his flock she had taken all his ghostly counsels as infallible; but now it seemed to him as though most of his words and many of his thoughts and actions were made subject by her to a bitter criticism. But in this matter he was inclined to rely much upon his own strength. Should he marry the lady, as he was still minded to do for many reasons, he would be to her a loving, careful husband; but he would also be her lord and master,—as was intended when marriage was made a holy ordinance. In this respect he did not doubt himself or his own powers. Hard words he could bear, and, as he thought, after a time control. So thinking, he was not disposed to allow the lady to recede from her troth to him, simply because in her anger she expressed a wish to do so. Therefore he had wisely been silent, and had shaken his head in reproach. But unfortunately the terms of their compact had not been finally settled with reference to another heading. Mrs. Prime had promised to be his wife, but she had burdened her promise with certain pecuniary conditions which were distasteful to him,—which were much opposed to that absolute headship and perfect mastery, which, as he thought, should belong to the husband as husband. His views on this subject were very strong, and he was by no means inclined to abate one jot of his demand. Better remain single in his work than accept the name of husband without its privileges! But he had hoped that by mingled firmness and gentle words he might bring his Dorothea round to a more womanly way of thinking. He had flattered himself that there was a power of eloquence in him which would have prevailed over her. Once or twice he thought that he was on the brink of success. He knew well that there were many points in his favour. A woman who has spoken of herself, and been spoken of, as being on the point of marriage, does not like to recede; and his Dorothea, though not specially womanly among women, was still a woman. Moreover he had the law on his side,—the old law as coming from the Scriptures. He could say that such a pecuniary arrangement as that proposed by his Dorothea was sinful. He had said so,—as he had then thought not without effect; but now she retaliated upon him with accusation of another sin! It was manifestly in her power to break away from him on that money detail. It seemed now to be her wish to break away from him; but she preferred doing so on that other matter. He began to fear that he must lose his wife, seeing that he was resolved never to yield on the money question; but he did not choose to be entrapped into an instant resignation of his engagement by Dorothea's indignation on a point of abstruse Scripturo-political morality. His Dorothea had assumed her indignation as a cloak for her pecuniary obstinacy. It might be that he must yield; but he would not surrender thus at the sound of a false summons. So he closed his eyes very pertinaciously and shook his head.

"I think upon the whole," said she again, "that we had better make up our minds to part." Then she stood up, feeling that she should thus employ a greater power in forcing an answer from him. He must have seen her motion through some cranny of his pertinaciously closed eyes, for he noticed it by rising from his own chair, with both his hands firmly fixed upon the table; but still he did not open his eyes, —unless it might be to the extent of that small cranny.

"Good-bye, Mr. Prong," said she.

Then he altered the form of his hands, and taking them from the table he dashed them together before his face. "God bless you, Dorothea!" said he. "God bless you! God bless you!" And he put out his hands as though blessing her in his darkness. She, perceiving the inutility of endeavouring to shake hands with a man who wouldn't open his eyes, moved away from her chair towards the door, purposely raising a sound of motion with her dress, so that he might know that she was going. In that I think she took an unnecessary precaution, for the cranny at the corner of his eye was still at his disposal.

"Good-bye, Mr. Prong," she said again, as she opened the door for herself.

"God bless you, Dorothea!" said he. "May God bless you!"

Then, without assistance at the front door she made her way out into the street, and as she stepped along the pavement, she formed a resolve, — which no eloquence from Mr. Prong could ever overcome, —that she would remain a widow for the rest of her days.

At twelve o'clock on the morning of the election Mr. Hart was declared by his own committee to be nine ahead, and was admitted to be six ahead by Mr. Cornbury's committee. But the Cornbury folk asserted confidently that in this they saw certain signs of success. Their supporters were not men who could be whipped up to the poll early in the day, whereas Hart's voters were all, more or less, under control, and had been driven up hurriedly to the hustings so as to make this early show of numbers. Mr. Hart was about everywhere speaking, and so was Butler Cornbury; but in the matter of oratory I am bound to acknowledge that the Jew had by much the mastery over the Christian. There are a class of men, —or rather more than a class, a section of mankind, —to whom a power of easy expression by means of spoken words comes naturally. English country gentlemen, highly educated as they are, undaunted as they usually are, self-confident as they in truth are at the bottom, are clearly not in this section. Perhaps they are further removed from it, considering the advantages they have for such speaking, than any other class of men in England, —or I might almost say elsewhere. The fact, for it is a fact, that some of the greatest orators whom the world has known have been found in this class, does not in any degree affect the truth of my proposition. The best grapes in the world are perhaps grown in England, though England is not a land of grapes. And for the same reason. The value of the thing depends upon its rarity, and its value instigates the efforts for excellence. The power of vocal expression which seems naturally to belong to an American is to an ordinary Englishman very marvellous; but in America the talking man is but little esteemed. "Very wonderful power of delivery,—that of Mr. So-and-So," says the Englishman, speaking of an American.

"Guess we don't think much of that kind of thing here," says the Yankee. "There's a deal too much of that coin in circulation."

English country gentlemen are not to be classed among that section of mankind which speaks easily in public, but Jews, I think, may be so classed. The men who speak thus easily and with natural fluency, are also they who learn languages easily. They are men who observe rather than think, who remember rather than create, who may not have great mental powers, but are ever ready with what they have, whose best word is at their command at a moment, and is then serviceable though perhaps incapable of more enduring service.

At any rate, as regarded oratory in Baslehurst the dark little man with the bright new hat from London was very much stronger than his opponent,—so much stronger that poor Butler Cornbury began to sicken of elections and to wish himself comfortably at home at Cornbury Grange. He knew that he was talking himself down while the Israelitish clothier was talking himself up. "It don't matter," Honyman said to him comfortably. "It's only done for the show of the thing and to fill up the day. If Gladstone were here he wouldn't talk a vote out of them one way or the other;—nor yet the devil himself." This consoled Butler Cornbury, but nevertheless he longed that the day might be over.

And Tappitt spoke too more than once,—as did also Luke Rowan, in spite of various noisy interruptions in which he was told that he was not an elector, and in spite also of an early greeting with a dead cat. Tappitt, in advocating the claims of Mr. Hart to be returned to Parliament as member for Baslehurst, was clever enough to introduce the subject of his own wrongs. And so important had this brewery question become that he was listened to with every sign of interest when he told the people for how many years Bungall and Tappitt had brewed beer for them, there in Baslehurst. Doubtless he was met by sundry interruptions from the Rowanites.

"What sort of tipple has it been, T.?" was demanded by one voice.

"Do you call that beer?" said a second.

"Where do you buy your hops?" asked a third.

But he went on manfully, and was buoyed up by a strong belief that he was fighting his own battle with success.

Nor was Rowan slow to answer him. He was proud to say that he was Bungall's heir, and as such he intended to continue Bungall's business. Whether he could improve the quality of the old tap he didn't know, but he would try. People had said a few weeks ago that he had been hounded out of Baslehurst, and did not mean to come back again. Here he was. He had bought property in Baslehurst. He meant to live in Baslehurst. He pledged himself to brew beer in Baslehurst. He already regarded himself as belonging to Baslehurst. And, being a bachelor, he hoped that he might live to marry a wife out of Baslehurst. This last assurance was received with unqualified applause from both factions, and went far in obtaining for Rowan that local popularity which was needful to him. Certainly the Rowan contest added much to the popular interest of that election.

At the close of the poll on that evening it was declared by the mayor that Mr. Butler Cornbury had been elected to serve the borough in Parliament by a majority of one vote.

CHAPTER X
THE BASLEHURST GAZETTE

By one vote! Old Mr. Cornbury when he heard of it gasped with dismay, and in secret regretted that his son had not been beaten. What seat could be gained by one vote and not be contested, especially when the beaten candidate was a Jew clothier rolling in money? And what sums would not a petition and scrutiny cost? Butler Cornbury himself was dismayed, and could hardly participate in the exultation of his more enthusiastic wife. Mr. Hart of course declared that he would petition, and that he was as sure of the seat as though he already occupied it. But as it was known that every possible electioneering device had been put in practice on his behalf during the last two hours of the poll, the world at large in Baslehurst believed that young Cornbury's position was secure. Tappitt and some few others were of a different opinion. At the present moment Tappitt could not endure to acknowledge to himself that he had been beaten. Nothing but the prestige and inward support of immediate success could support him in that contest, so much more important to himself, in which he was now about to be engaged. That matter of the petition, however, can hardly be brought into the present story. The political world will understand that it would be carried on with great vigour.

The news of the election of Butler Cornbury reached the cottage at Bragg's End by the voice of Mr. Sturt on the same evening; and Mrs. Ray, in her quiet way, expressed much joy that Mr. Comfort's son-in-law should have been successful, and that Baslehurst should not have disgraced itself by any connexion with a Jew. To her it had appeared monstrous that such a one should have been even permitted to show himself in the town as a candidate for its representation. To such she would have denied all civil rights, and almost all social rights. For a true spirit of persecution one should always go to a woman; and the milder, the sweeter, the more loving, the more womanly the woman, the stronger will be that spirit within her. Strong love for the thing loved necessitates strong hatred for the thing hated, and thence comes the spirit of persecution. They in England who are now keenest against the Jews, who would again take from them rights that they have lately won, are certainly those who think most of the faith of a Christian. The most deadly enemies of the Roman Catholics are they who love best their religion as Protestants. When we look to individuals we always find it so, though it hardly suits us to admit as much when we discuss these subjects broadly. To Mrs. Ray it was wonderful that a Jew should have been entertained in Baslehurst as a future member for the borough, and that he should have been admitted to speak aloud within a few yards of the church tower!

On the day but one after the election Mrs. Sturt brought over to the cottage an extra sheet of the "Baslehurst Gazette," which had been published out of its course, and which was devoted to the circumstances of the election. I am not sure that Mrs. Sturt would have regarded this somewhat dull report of the election speeches as having any peculiar interest for Mrs. Ray and her daughter had it not been for one special passage. Luke Rowan's speech about Baslehurst was given at length, and in it was contained that public promise as to his matrimonial intentions. Mrs. Sturt came into the cottage parlour with the paper doubled into four, and with her finger on a particular spot. To her it had seemed that Rowan's promise must have been intended for Rachel, and it seemed also that nothing could be more manly, straightforward, or gallant than that assurance. It suited her idea of chivalry. But she was not quite sure that Rachel would enjoy the publicity of the declaration, and therefore she was prepared to point the passage out more particularly to Mrs. Ray. "I've brought 'ee the account of it all," said she, still holding the paper in her hand. "The gudeman,—he's done with t' paper, and you'll keep it for good and all. One young man that we know of has made t' finest speech of 'em all to my mind. Luik at that, Mrs. Ray." Then, with a knowing wink at the mother, and a poke at the special words with her finger, she left the sheet in Mrs. Ray's hand, and went her way.

Mrs. Ray, who had not quite understood the pantomime, and whose eye had not caught the words relating to marriage, saw however that the column indicated contained the report of a speech made by Luke Rowan, and she began it at the beginning and read it throughout. Luke had identified himself with the paper, and therefore received from it almost more than justice. His words were given at very full length, and for some ten minutes she was reading before she came to the words which Mrs. Sturt had hoped would be so delightful.

"What is it, mamma?" Rachel asked.

"A speech, my dear, made at the election."

"And who made it, mamma?"

Mrs. Ray hesitated for a moment before she answered, thereby letting Rachel know full well who made the speech before the word was spoken. But at last she did speak the word—"Mr. Rowan, my dear."

"Oh!" said Rachel; she longed to get hold of the newspaper, but she would utter no word expressive of such longing. Since that evening on which she had been bidden to look at the clouds she had regarded Luke as a special hero, cleverer than other men around her, as a man born to achieve things and make himself known. It was not astonishing to her that a speech of his should be reported at length in the newspaper. He was a man certain to rise, to make speeches, and to be reported. So she thought of him; and so thinking had almost wished that it were not so. Could she expect that such a one would stoop to her? or that if he did so that she could be fit for him? He had now perceived that himself, and therefore had taken her at her word, and had left her. Had he been more like other men around her;— more homely, less prone to rise, with less about him of fire and genius, she might have won him and kept him. The prize would not have been so precious; but still, she thought, it might have been sufficient for her heart. A young man who could find printers and publishers to report his words in that way, on the first moment of his coming among them, would he turn aside from his path to look after her? Would he not bring with him some grand lady down from London as his wife?

"Dear me!" said Mrs. Ray, quite startled. "Oh, dear! What do you think he says?"

"What does he say, mamma?"

"Well, I don't know. Perhaps he mayn't mean it. I don't think I ought to have spoken of it."

"If it's in the newspaper I suppose I should have heard of it, unless you sent it back without letting me see it."

"She said we were to keep it, and it's because of that, I'm sure. She was always the most good-natured woman in the world. I don't know what we should have done if we hadn't found such a neighbour as Mrs. Sturt."

"But what is it, mamma, that you are speaking of in the newspapers?"

"Mr. Rowan says—Oh, dear! I wish I'd let you come to it yourself. How very odd that he should get up and say that kind of thing in public before all the people. He says;—but any way I know he means it because he's so honest. And after all if he means it, it doesn't much matter where he says it. Handsome is that handsome does. There, my dear; I don't know how to tell it you, so you had better read it yourself."

Rachel with eager hands took the paper, and began the speech as her mother had done, and read it through. She read it through till she came to those words, and then she put the paper down beside her. "I understand what you mean, mamma, and what Mrs. Sturt meant; but Mr. Rowan did not mean that."

"What did he mean, my dear?"

"He meant them to understand that he intended to become a man of Baslehurst like one of themselves."

"But then why did he talk about finding a wife there?"

"He wouldn't have said that, mamma, if he had meant anything particular. If anything of that sort had been at all in his mind, it would have kept him from saying what he did say."

"But didn't he mean that he intended to marry a Baslehurst lady?"

"He meant it in that sort of way in which men do mean such things. It was his way to make them think well of him. But don't let us talk any more about it, mamma. It isn't nice."

"Well, I'm sure I can't understand it," said Mrs. Ray. But she became silent on the subject, and the reading of the newspaper was passed over to Rachel.

This had not been completed when a step was heard on the gravel walk outside, and Mrs. Ray, jumping up, declared it to be the step of her eldest daughter. It was so, and Mrs. Prime was very soon in the room. It was at this time about four o'clock in the afternoon, and therefore, as the hour for tea at the cottage was half-past five, it was naturally understood that Mrs. Prime had come there to join them at their evening meal. After their first greeting she had seated herself on the sofa, and there was that in her manner which showed both to her mother and sister that she was somewhat confused,— that she had something to say as to which there was some hesitation. "Do take off your bonnet, Dorothea," said her mother.

"Will you come up-stairs, Dolly," said her sister, "and put your hair straight after your walk?"

But Dolly did not care whether her hair was straight or tossed, as the Irish girls say when the smoothness of their locks has been disarranged. She took off her bonnet, however, and laid it on the sofa beside her. "Mother," she said, "I've got something particular that I want to say to you."

"I hope it's not anything serious the matter," said Mrs. Ray.

"Well, mother, it is serious. Things are serious mostly, I think,—or should be."

"Shall I go into the garden while you are speaking to mamma?" said Rachel.

"No, Rachel; not on my account. What I've got to say should be said to you as well as to mother. It's all over between me and Mr. Prong."

"No!" said Mrs. Ray.

"I thought it would be," said Rachel.

"And why did you think so?" said Mrs. Prime, turning round upon her sister, almost angrily.

"I felt that he wouldn't suit you, Dolly; that's why I thought so. If it's all over now, I suppose there's no harm in saying that I didn't like him well enough to hope he'd be my brother-in-law."

"But that couldn't make you think it. However, it's all over between us. We agreed that it should be so this morning; and I thought it right to come out and let you know at once."

"I'm glad you've told us," said Mrs. Ray.

"Was there any quarrel?" asked Rachel.

"No, Rachel, there was no quarrel; not what you call a quarrel, I suppose. We found there were subjects of disagreement between us,—matters on which we had adverse opinions; and therefore it was better that we should part."

"It was about the money, perhaps?" said Mrs. Ray.

"Well, yes; it was in part about the money. Had I known then as much as I do now about the law in such matters, I should have told Mr. Prong from the first that it could not be. He is a good man, and I hope I have not disturbed his happiness."

"I used to be afraid that he would disturb yours," said Rachel, "and therefore I cannot pretend to regret it."

"That's not charitable, Rachel. But if you please we won't say anything more about it. It's over, and that is enough. And now, mother, I want to know if you will object to my returning here and living at the cottage again."

Mrs. Ray could not bethink herself at the moment what answer she might best make, and therefore for some moments she made none. For herself she would have been delighted that her eldest daughter should return to the cottage. Under no circumstances could she refuse her own child a home under her own roof. But at the present moment she could not forget the circumstances under which Mrs. Prime had gone, and it militated sorely against Mrs. Ray's sense of justice that the return should be made to depend on other circumstances. Mrs. Prime had gone away in loud disapproval of Rachel's conduct; and now she proposed to return, on this breaking up of her own matrimonial arrangements, as though she had left the cottage because of her proposed marriage. Mrs. Prime should be welcomed back, but her return should be accompanied by a withdrawal of her accusation against Rachel. Mrs. Ray did not know how to put her demand into words, but her mind was clear on the subject.

"Well, mother," said Mrs. Prime; "is there any objection?"

"No, my dear; no objection at all: of course not. I shall be delighted to have you back, and so, I'm sure, will Rachel; but—"

"But what? Is it about money?"

"Oh, dear, no! Nothing about money at all. If you do come back,—and I'm sure I hope you will; and indeed it seems quite unnatural that you should be staying in Baslehurst, while we are living here. But I think you ought to say, my dear, that Rachel behaved just as she ought to behave in all that matter about,—about Mr. Rowan, you know."

"Don't mind me, mamma," said Rachel,—who could, however, have smothered her mother with kisses, on hearing these words.

"But I think we all ought to understand each other, Rachel. You and your sister can't go on comfortably together, if there's to be more black looks about that."

"I don't know that there have been any black looks," said Mrs. Prime, looking very black as she spoke.

"At any rate we should understand each other," continued Mrs. Ray, with admirable courage. "I've thought a great deal about it since you've been away. Indeed I haven't thought about much else. And I don't think I shall ever forgive myself for having let a hard word be said to Rachel about it."

"Oh, mamma, don't,—don't," said Rachel. But those meditated embraces were continued in her imagination.

"I don't want to say any hard words," said Mrs. Prime.

"No; I'm sure you don't;—only they were said,—weren't they, now? Didn't we blame her about being out there in the churchyard that evening?"

"Mamma!" exclaimed Rachel.

"Well, my dear, I won't say any more;—only this. Your sister went away because she thought you weren't good enough for her to live with; and if she comes back again,—which I'm sure I hope she will,—I think she ought to say that she's been mistaken."

Mrs. Prime looked very black, and no word fell from her. She sat there silent and gloomy, while Mrs. Ray looked at the fireplace, lost in wonder at her own effort. Whether she would have given way or not, had she and Mrs. Prime been alone, I cannot say. That Mrs. Prime would have uttered no outspoken recantation I feel sure. It was Rachel at last who settled the matter.

"If Dolly comes back to live here, mamma," said she, "I shall take that as an acknowledgment on her part that she thinks I am good enough to live with."

"Well, my dear," said Mrs. Ray, "perhaps that'll do; only there should be an understanding, you know."

Mrs. Prime at the moment said nothing; but when next she spoke her words showed her intention of having her things brought back to the cottage on the next day. I think it must be felt that Rachel had won the victory. She felt it so herself, and was conscious that no further attempt would be made to carry her off to Dorcas meetings against her own will.

CHAPTER XI
CORNBURY GRANGE

Luke Rowan had been told that Mrs. Butler Cornbury wished to see him when the election should be over; and on the evening of the election the victorious candidate, before he returned home, asked Luke to come to the Grange on the following Monday and stay till the next Wednesday. Now it must be understood that Rowan during this period of the election had become, in a public way, very intimate with Cornbury. They were both young men, the new Member of Parliament not being over thirty, and for the time they were together employed on the same matter. Luke Rowan was one with whom such a man as Mr. Cornbury could not zealously co-operate without reaching a considerable extent of personal intimacy. He was pleasant-mannered, free in speech, with a bold eye, assuming though not asserting his equality with the best of those with whom he might be brought in contact. Had Cornbury chosen to consider himself by reason of his social station too high for Rowan's fellowship, he might of course have avoided him; but he could not have put himself into close contact with the man, without submitting himself to that temporary equality which Rowan assumed, and to that temporary familiarity which sprung from it. Butler Cornbury had thought little about it. He had found Rowan to be a pleasant associate and an able assistant, and had fallen into that mode of fellowship which the other man's ways and words had made natural to him. When his wife begged him to ask Rowan up to the Grange, he had been startled for a moment, but had at once assented.

"Well," said he; "he's an uncommon pleasant fellow. I don't see why he shouldn't come."

"I've a particular reason," said Mrs. Butler.

"All right," said the husband. "Do you explain it to my father." And so the invitation had been given.

But Rowan was a man more thoughtful than Cornbury, and was specially thoughtful as to his own position. He was a radical at heart if ever there was a radical. But in saying this I must beg my reader to understand that a radical is not necessarily a revolutionist or even a republican. He does not, by reason of his social or political radicalism, desire the ruin of thrones, the degradation of nobles, the spoliation of the rich, or even the downfall of the bench of bishops. Many a young man is frightened away from the just conclusions of his mind and the strong convictions of his heart by dread of being classed with those who are jealous of the favoured ones of fortune. A radical may be as ready as any aristocrat to support the crown with his blood, and the church with his faith. It is in this that he is a radical; that he desires, expects, works for, and believes in, the gradual progress of the people. No doctrine of equality is his. Liberty he must have, and such position, high or low, for himself and others, as each man's individual merits will achieve for him. The doctrine of outward equality he eschews as a barrier to all ambition, and to all improvement. The idea is as mean as the thing is impracticable. But within,—is it in his soul or in his heart?—within his breast there is a manhood that will own no inferiority to the manhood of another. He retires to a corner that an earl with his suite may pass proudly through the doorway, and he grudges the earl nothing of his pride. It is the earl's right. But he also has his right; and neither queen, nor earl, nor people shall invade it. That is the creed of a radical.

Rowan, as I have said, was a man thoughtful as to his own position. He had understood well the nature of the league between himself and Butler Cornbury. It was his intention to become a brewer in Baslehurst; and a brewer in Baslehurst would by no means be as the mighty brewers of great name, who marry lord's daughters, and give their daughters in marriage to mighty lords. He would simply be a tradesman in the town. It might well be that he should not find the society of the Tappitts and the Griggses much to his taste, but such as it was he would make the best of it. At any rate he would make no attempt to force his way into other society. If others came to him let that be their look out. Now, when Cornbury asked him thus to come to Cornbury Grange, as though they two were men living in the same class of life,—as though they were men who might be bound together socially in their homes as well as politically on the hustings, the red colour came to his face and he hesitated for a moment in his answer.

"You are very kind," said he.

"Oh! you must come," said Cornbury. "My wife particularly desires it."

"She is very kind," said he. "But if you ask all your supporters over to the Grange you'll get rather a mixed lot."

"I suppose I should; but I don't mean to do that. I shall be very glad, however, to see you;—very glad."

"And I shall be very happy to come," said Rowan, having again hesitated as he gave his answer.

"I wish I hadn't promised that I'd go there," he said to himself afterwards. This was on the Sunday, after evening church,—an hour or more after the people had all gone home, and he was sitting on that stile, looking to the west, and thinking, as he looked, of that sunset which he and another had seen as they stood there together. He did wish that he had not undertaken to go to Mr. Cornbury's house. What to him would be the society of such people as he should find there,—to him who had laid out for himself a career that would necessarily place his life among other associates? "I'll send and excuse myself," he said. "I'll be called away to Exeter. I have things to do there. I shall only get into a mess by knowing people who will drop me when this ferment of the election is over." And yet the idea of an intimacy at such a house as Cornbury Grange,—with such people as Mrs. Butler Cornbury, was very sweet to him; only this, that if he associated with them or such as them it must be on equal terms. He could acknowledge them to be people apart from him, as ice creams and sponge cakes are things apart from the shillingless schoolboy. But as the schoolboy, if brought within the range of cakes and creams, must devour them with unchecked relish, as though his pocket were lined with coin; so must he, Rowan, carry himself with these curled darlings of society if he found himself placed among them. He liked cakes and creams, but had made up his mind that other viands were as wholesome and more comfortably within his reach. Was it worth his while to go to this banquet which would unsettle his taste, and at which perhaps if he sat there at his ease, he might not be wholly welcome? All his thoughts were not noble. He had declared to himself that a certain thing could not be his except at a cost which he would not pay, and yet he hankered for that thing. He had declared to himself that no social position in which he might ever find himself should make a change in him, on his inner self or on his outward manner; and now he feared to go among these people, lest he should find himself an inferior among superiors. It was not all noble; but there was beneath it a basis of nobility. "I will go," he said at last, fearing that if he did not, there would have been some grain of cowardice in the motives of his action. "If they don't like me it's their fault for asking me."

Of course as he sat there he was thinking of Rachel. Of course he had thought of Rachel daily, almost hourly, since he had been with her at the cottage, when she had bent her head over his shoulder, and submitted to have his arm round her waist. But his thoughts of her were not as hers of him. Nor is it often that a man's love is like a woman's,—restless, fearful, uncomfortable, sleepless, timid, and all-pervading. Not the less may it be passionate, constant, and faithful. He had been angered by Rachel's letter to him,—greatly angered. Of a truth when Mrs. Ray met him in Exeter he had no message to send back to Cawston. He had done his part, and had been rejected;—had been rejected too clearly because on the summing up of his merits and demerits at the cottage, his demerits had been found to be the heavier. He did not suspect that the calculation had been made by Rachel herself; and therefore he had never said to himself that all should be over between them. He had never determined that there should be a quarrel between them. But he was angered, and he would stand aloof from her. He would stand aloof from her, and would no longer acknowledge that he was in any way bound by the words he had spoken. All such bonds she had broken. Nevertheless I think he loved her with a surer love after receiving that letter than he had ever felt before.

He had been here, at this spot, every evening since his return to Baslehurst; and here had thought much of his future life, and something, too, of the days that were past. Looking to the left he could see the trees that stood in front of the old brewery, hiding the building from his eyes. That was the house in which old Bungall had lived, and there Tappitt had lived for the last twenty years. "I suppose," said he, speaking to himself, "it will be my destiny to live there too, with the vats and beer barrels under my nose. But what farmer ever throve who disliked the muck of his own farm-yard?" Then he had thought of Tappitt and of the coming battle, and had laughed as he remembered the scene with the poker. At that moment his eye caught the bright colours of women's bonnets coming into the field beneath him, and he knew that the Tappitt girls were returning home from their walk. He had retired quickly round the chancel of the church, and had watched, thinking that Rachel would be with them. But Rachel, of course, was not there. He said to himself that they had thrown her off; and said also that the time should come when they should be glad to win from her a kind word and an encouraging smile. His love for Rachel was as true and more strong than ever; but it was of that nature that he was able to tell himself that it had for the present moment been set aside by her act, and that it became him to leave it for a while in abeyance.

"What on earth shall I do with myself all Tuesday?" he said again as he walked away from the churchyard on the Sunday evening. "I don't know what these people do with themselves when there's no hunting and shooting. It seems unnatural to me that a man shouldn't have his bread to earn,—or a woman either in some form." After that he went back to his inn.

On the Monday he went out to Cornbury Grange late in the afternoon. Butler Cornbury drove into Baslehurst with a pair of horses, and took him back in his phaeton.

"Give my fellow your portmanteau. That's all right. You never were at the Grange, were you? It's the prettiest five miles of a drive in Devonshire;

but the walk along the river is the prettiest walk in England,—which is saying a great deal more."

"I know the walk well," said Rowan, "though I never was inside the park."

"It isn't much of a park. Indeed there isn't a semblance of a park about it. Grange is just the name for it, as it's an upper-class sort of homestead for a gentleman farmer. We've lived there since long before Adam, but we've never made much of a house of it."

"That's just the sort of place that I should like to have myself."

"If you had it you wouldn't be content. You'd want to pull down the house and build a bigger one. It's what I shall do some day, I suppose. But if I do it will never be so pretty again. I suppose that fellow will petition; won't he?"

"I should say he would;—though he won't get anything by it."

"He knows his purse is longer than ours, and he'll think to frighten us;—and, by George, he will frighten us too! My father is not a rich man by any means."

"You should stand to your guns now."

"I mean to do so, if I can. My wife's father is made of money."

"What! Mr. Comfort?"

"Yes. He's been blessed with the most surprising number of unmarried uncles and aunts that ever a man had. He's rather fond of me, and likes the idea of my being in Parliament. I think I shall hint to him that he must pay for the idea. Here we are. Will you come and take a turn round the place before dinner?"

Rowan was then taken into the house and introduced to the old squire, who received him with the stiff urbanity of former days.

"You are welcome to the Grange, Mr. Rowan. You'll find us very quiet here; which is more, I believe, than can have been said of Baslehurst these last two or three days. My daughter-in-law is somewhere with the children. She'll be here before dinner. Butler, has that tailor fellow gone back to London yet?"

Butler told his father that the tailor had at least gone away from Baslehurst; and then the two younger men went out and walked about the grounds till dinner time.

It was Mrs. Butler Cornbury who gave soul and spirit to daily life at Cornbury Grange,—who found the salt with which the bread was quickened, and the wine with which the heart was made glad. Marvellous is the power which can be exercised, almost unconsciously, over a company, or an individual, or even upon a crowd by one person gifted with good temper, good digestion, good intellects, and good looks. A woman so endowed charms not only by the exercise of her own gifts, but she endows those who are near her with a sudden conviction that it is they whose temper, health, talents, and appearance is doing so much for society. Mrs. Butler Cornbury was such a woman as this. The Grange was a popular house. The old squire was not found to be very dull. The young squire was thought to be rather clever. The air of the house was lively and bracing. Men and women did not find the days there to be over long. And Mrs. Butler Cornbury did it all.

Rowan did not see her till he met her in the drawing-room, just before dinner, when he found that two or three other ladies were also staying there. She came up to him when he entered the room, and greeted him as though he were an old friend. All conversation at that moment of course had reference to the election. Thanks were given and congratulations received; and when old Mr. Cornbury shook his head, his daughter-in-law assured him that there would be nothing to fear.

"I don't know what you call nothing to fear, my dear. I call two thousand pounds a great deal to fear."

"I shouldn't wonder if we don't hear another word about him," said she.

The old man uttered a long sigh. "It seems to me," said he, "that no gentleman ought to stand for a seat in Parliament since these people have been allowed to come up. Purity of election, indeed! It makes me sick. Come along, my dear." Then he gave his arm to one of the young ladies, and toddled into the dining-room.

Mrs. Butler Cornbury said nothing special to Luke Rowan on that evening, but she made the hours very pleasant to him. All those half-morbid ideas as to social difference between himself and his host's family soon vanished. The house was very comfortable, the girls were very pretty, Mrs. Cornbury was very kind, and everything went very well. On the following morning it was nearly ten when they sat down to breakfast, and half the morning before lunch had passed away in idle chat before the party bethought itself of what it should do for the day. At last it was agreed that they would all stroll out through the woods up to a special reach of the river which there ran through a ravine of rock, called Cornbury Cleeves. Many in those parts declared that Cornbury Cleeves was the prettiest spot in England. I am not prepared to bear my testimony to the truth of that very wide assertion. I can only say that I know no prettier spot. The river here was rapid and sparkling; not rapid because driven into small compass, for its breadth was greater and more regular in its passage through the Cleeves than it was either above or below, but rapid from the declivity of its course. On one side the rocks came sheer down to the water, but on the other there was a strip of meadow, or rather a grassy amphitheatre, for the wall of rocks at the back of it was semi-circular, so as to enclose the field on every side. There might be four or five acres of green meadow here; but the whole was so interspersed with old stunted oak trees and thorns standing alone that the space looked larger than it was. The rocks on each side were covered here and there with the richest foliage; and the spot might be taken to be a valley from which, as from that of Rasselas, there was no escape. Down close upon the margin of the water a bathing-house had been built, from which a plunge could be taken into six or seven feet of the coolest, darkest, cleanest water that a bather could desire in his heart.

"I suppose you never were here before," said Mrs. Cornbury to Rowan.

"Indeed I have," said he. "I always think it such a grand thing that you landed magnates can't keep all your delights to yourself. I dare say I've been here oftener than you have during the last three months."

"That's very likely, seeing that it's my first visit this summer."

"And I've been here a dozen times. I suppose you'll think I'm a villanous trespasser when I tell you that I've bathed in that very house more than once."

"Then you've done more than I ever did; and yet we had it made thinking it would do for ladies. But the water looks so black."

"Ah! I like that, as long as it's a clear black."

"I like bathing where I can see the bright stones like jewels at the bottom. You can never do that in fresh water. It's only in some nook of the sea, where there is no sand, when the wind outside has died away, and when the tide is quiet and at its full. Then one can drop gently in and almost fancy that one belongs to the sea as the mermaids do. I wonder how the idea of mermaids first came?"

"Some one saw a crowd of young women bathing."

"But then how came they to have looking-glasses and fishes' tails?"

"The fishes' tails were taken as granted because they were in the sea, and the looking-glasses because they were women," said Rowan.

"And the one with as much reason as the other. By-the-by, Mr. Rowan, talking of women, and fishes' tails, and looking-glasses, and all other feminine attractions, when did you see Miss Ray last?"

Rowan paused before he answered her, and looking round perceived that he had strayed with Mrs. Cornbury to the furthest end of the meadow, away from their companions. It immediately came across his mind that this was the matter on which Mrs. Cornbury wished to speak to him, and by some combative process he almost resolved that he would not be spoken to on that matter.

"When did I see Miss Ray?" said he, repeating her question. "Two or three days after Mrs. Tappitt's party. I have not seen her since that."

"And why don't you go and see her?" said Mrs. Cornbury.

Now this was asked him in a tone which made it necessary that he should either answer her question or tell her simply that he would not answer it. The questioner's manner was so firm, so eager, so incisive, that the question could not be turned away.

"I am not sure that I am prepared to tell you," said he.

"Ah! but I want you to be prepared," said she; "or rather, perhaps, to tell the truth, I want to drive you to an answer without preparation. Is it not true that you made her an offer, and that she accepted it?"

Rowan thought a moment, and then he answered her, "It is true."

"I should not have asked the question if I had not positively known that such was the case. I have never spoken a word to her about it, and yet I knew it. Her mother told my father."

"Well?"

"And as that is so, why do you not go and see her? I am sure you are not one of those who would play such a trick as that upon such a girl with the mere purpose of amusing yourself."

"Upon no girl would I do so, Mrs. Cornbury."

"I feel sure of it. Therefore why do you not go to her?" They walked along together for a few minutes under the rocks in silence, and then Mrs. Cornbury again repeated her question, "Why do you not go to her?"

"Mrs. Cornbury," he said, "you must not be angry with me if I say that that is a matter which at the present moment I am not willing to discuss."

"Nor must you be angry with me if, as Rachel's friend, I say something further about it. As you do not wish to answer me, I will ask no other question; but at any rate you will be willing to listen to me. Rachel has never spoken to me on this subject—not a word; but I know from others who see her daily that she is very unhappy."

"I am grieved that it should be so."

"Yes, I knew you would be grieved. But how could it be otherwise? A girl, you know, Mr. Rowan, has not other things to occupy her mind as a man has. I think of Rachel Ray that she would have been as happy there at Bragg's End as the day is long, if no offer of love had come in her way. She was not a girl whose head had been filled with romance, and who looked for such things. But for that very reason is she less able to bear the loss of it when the offer has come in her way. I think, perhaps, you hardly know the depth of her character and the strength of her love."

"I think I know that she is constant."

"Then why do you try her so hardly?"

Mrs. Cornbury had promised that she would ask no more questions; but the asking of questions was her easiest mode of saying that which she had to say. And Rowan, though he had declared that he would answer no question, could hardly avoid the necessity of doing so.

"It may be that the trial is the other way."

"I know;—I understand. They made her write a letter to you. It was my father's doing. I will tell you the whole truth. It was my father's doing, and therefore it is that I think myself bound to speak to you. Her mother came to him for advice, and he had heard evil things spoken of you in Baslehurst. You will see that I am very frank with you. And I will take some credit to myself too. I believed such tidings to be altogether false, and I made inquiry which proved that I was right. But my father had given the advice which he thought best. I do not know what Rachel wrote to you, but a girl's letter under such circumstances can hardly do more than express the will of those who guide her. It was sad enough for her to be forced to write such a letter, but it will be sadder still if you cannot be brought to forgive it."

Then she paused, standing under the gray rock and looking up eagerly into his face. But he made her no answer, nor gave her any sign. His heart was very tender at that moment towards Rachel, but there was that in him of the stubbornness of manhood which would not let him make any sign of his tenderness.

"I will not press you to say anything, Mr. Rowan," she continued, "and I am much obliged to you for having listened to me. I've known Rachel Ray for many years, and that must be my excuse."

"No excuse is wanting," he said. "If I do not say anything it is not because I am offended. There are things on which a man should not allow himself to speak without considering them."

"Oh, certainly. Come; shall we go back to them at the bathing-house? They'll think we've lost ourselves."

Thus Mrs. Cornbury said the words which she had desired to speak on Rachel Ray's behalf.

When they reached the Grange there were still two hours left before the time of dressing for dinner should come, and during these hours Luke returned by himself to the Cleeves. He escaped from his host, and retraced his steps, and on reaching the river sat himself down on the margin, and looked into the cool dark running water. Had he been severe to Rachel? He would answer no such question when asked by Mrs. Cornbury, but he was very desirous of answering it to himself. The women at the cottage had doubted him,—Mrs. Ray and her daughter, with perhaps that other daughter of whom he had only heard; and he had resolved that they should see him no more and hear of him no more till there should be no further room for doubt. Then he would show himself again at the cottage, and again ask Rachel to be his wife. There was some manliness in this; but there was also a hardness in his pride which deserved the rebuke which Mrs. Cornbury's words had conveyed to him. He had been severe to Rachel. Lying there, with his full length stretched upon the grass, he acknowledged to himself that he had thought more of his own feelings than of hers. While Mrs. Cornbury had been speaking he could not bring himself to feel that this was the case. But now in his solitude he did acknowledge it. What amount of sin had she committed against him that she should be so punished by him who loved her? He took out her letter from his pocket, and found that her words were loving, though she had not been allowed to put into them that eager, pressing, speaking love which he had desired.

"Spoken ill of me, have they?" said he to himself, as he got up to walk back to the Grange. "Well, that was natural too. What an ass a man is to care for such things as that!"

On that evening and the next morning the Cornburys were very gracious to him; and then he returned to Baslehurst, on the whole well pleased with his visit.

CHAPTER XII
IN WHICH THE QUESTION OF
THE BREWERY IS SETTLED

During the day or two immediately subsequent to the election, Mr. Tappitt found himself to be rather downhearted. The excitement of the contest was over. He was no longer buoyed up by the consoling and almost triumphant assurances of success for himself against his enemy Rowan, which had been administered to him by those with whom he had been acting on behalf of Mr. Hart. He was alone and thoughtful in his counting-house, or else subjected to the pressure of his wife's arguments in his private dwelling. He had never yet been won over to say that he would agree to any proposition, but he knew that he must now form some decision. Rowan would not even wait till the lawsuit should be decided by legal means. If Mr. Tappitt would not consent to one of the three propositions made to him, Rowan would at once commence the building of his new brewery. "He is that sort of man," said Honyman, "that if he puts a brick down nothing in the world will prevent him from going on."

"Of course it won't," said Mrs. Tappitt. "Oh dear, oh dear, T.! if you go on in this way we shall all be ruined; and then people will say that it was my fault, and that I ought to have had you inquired into about your senses."

Tappitt gnashed his teeth and rushed out of the dining-room back into his brewery. Among all those who were around him there was not one to befriend him. Even Worts had turned against him, and had received notice to go with a stern satisfaction which Tappitt had perfectly understood.

Tappitt was in this frame of mind, and was seated on his office stool, with his hat over his eyes, when he was informed by one of the boys about the place that a deputation from the town had come to wait upon him;—so he pulled off his hat, and begged that the deputation might be shown into the counting-house. The deputation consisted of three tradesmen who were desirous of convening a meeting with the view of discussing the petition against Mr. Cornbury's return to Parliament, and they begged that Mr. Tappitt would take the chair. The meeting was to be held at the Dragon, and it was proposed that after the meeting there should be a little dinner.

Mr. Tappitt would perhaps consent to take the chair at the dinner also. Mr. Tappitt did consent to both propositions, and when the deputation withdrew, he felt himself to be himself once more. His courage had returned to him, and he would at once rebuke his wife for the impropriety of the words she had addressed to him. He would rebuke his wife, and would then proceed to meet Mr. Sharpit the attorney, at the Dragon, and to take the chair at the meeting. It could not be that a young adventurer such as Rowan could put down an old-established firm, such as his own, or banish from the scene of his labours a man of such standing in the town as himself! It was all the fault of Honyman,—of Honyman who never was firm on any matter. When the meeting should be over he would say a word or two to Sharpit, and see if he could not put the matter into better training.

With a heavy tread, a tread that was intended to mark his determination, he ascended to the drawing-room and from thence to the bed-room above in which Mrs. Tappitt was then seated. She understood the meaning of the footfall, and knew well that it indicated a purpose of marital authority. A woman must have much less of natural wit than had fallen to Mrs. Tappitt's share, who has not learned from the experience of thirty years the meaning of such marital signs and sounds. So she sat herself firmly in her seat, caught hold of the petticoat which she was mending with a stout grasp, and prepared herself for the battle. "Margaret," said he, when he had carefully closed the door behind him, "I have come up to say that I do not intend to dine at home to-day."

"Oh, indeed," said she. "At the Dragon, I suppose then."

"Yes; at the Dragon. I've been asked to take the chair at a popular meeting which is to be held with reference to the late election."

"Take the chair!"

"Yes, my dear, take the chair at the meeting and at the dinner."

"Now, T., don't you make a fool of yourself."

"No, I won't; but Margaret, I must tell you once for all that that is not the way in which I like you to speak to me. Why you should have so much less confidence in my judgment than other people in Baslehurst, I cannot conceive; but—"

"Now, T., look here; as for your taking the chair as you call it, of course you can do it if you like it."

"Of course I can; and I do like it, and I mean to do it. But it isn't only about that I've come to speak to you. You said something to me to-day, before Honyman, that was very improper."

"What I say always is improper, I know."

"I don't suppose you could have intended to insinuate that you thought that I was a lunatic."

"I didn't say so."

"You said something like it."

"No, I didn't, T."

"Yes you did, Margaret."

"If you'll allow me for a moment, T., I'll tell you what I did say, and if you wish it, I'll say it again."

"No; I'd rather not hear it said again."

"But, T., I don't choose to be misunderstood, nor yet misrepresented."

"I haven't misrepresented you."

"But I say you have misrepresented me. If I ain't allowed to speak a word, of course it isn't any use for me to open my mouth. I hope I know what my duty is and I hope I've done it;—both by you, T., and by the children. I know I'm bound to submit, and I hope I have submitted. Very hard it has been sometimes when I've seen things going as they have gone; but I've remembered my duty as a wife, and I've held my tongue when any other woman in England would have spoken out. But there are some things which a woman can't stand and shouldn't; and if I'm to see my girls ruined and left without a roof over their heads, or a bit to eat, or a thing to wear, it shan't be for want of a word from me."

"Didn't they always have plenty to eat?"

"But where is it to come from if you're going to rush openmouthed into the lion's jaws in this way? I've done my duty by you, T., and no man nor yet no woman can say anything to the contrary. And if it was myself only I'd see myself on the brink of starvation before I'd say a word; but I can't see those poor girls brought to beggary without telling you what everybody in Baslehurst is talking about; and I can't see you, T., behaving in such a way and sit by and hold my tongue."

"Behave in what way? Haven't I worked like a horse? Do you mean to tell me that I am to give up my business, and my position, and everything I have in the world, and go away because a young scoundrel comes to Baslehurst and tells me that he wants to have my brewery? I tell you what, Margaret, if you think I'm that sort of man, you don't know me yet."

"I don't know about knowing you, T."

"No; you don't know me."

"If you come to that, I know very well that I have been deceived. I didn't want to speak of it, but now I must. I have been made to believe for these last twenty years that the brewery was all your own, whereas it now turns out that you've only got a share in it, and for aught I can see, by no means the best share. Why wasn't I told all that before?"

"Woman!" shouted Mr. Tappitt.

"Yes; woman indeed! I suppose I am a woman, and therefore I'm to have no voice in anything. Will you answer me one question, if you please? Are you going to that man, Sharpit?"

"Yes, I am."

"Then, Mr. Tappitt, I shall consult my brothers." Mrs. Tappitt's brothers were grocers in Plymouth; men whom Mr. Tappitt had never loved. "They mayn't hold their heads quite as high as you do,—or rather as you used to do when people thought that the establishment was all your own; but such as it is nobody can turn them out of their shop in the Market-place. If you are going to Sharpit, I shall consult them."

"You may consult the devil, if you like it."

"Oh, oh! very well, Mr. Tappitt. It's clear enough that you're not yourself any longer, and that somebody must take up your affairs and manage them for you. If you'll follow my advice you'll stay at home this evening and take a dose of physic and see Dr. Haustus quietly in the morning."

"I shall do nothing of the kind."

"Very well. Of course I can't make you. As yet you're your own master. If you choose to go to this silly meeting and then to drink gin and water and to smoke bad tobacco till all hours at the Dragon, and you in the dangerous state you are at present, I can't help it. I don't suppose that anything I could do now, that is quite immediately, would enable me to put you under fitting restraint."

"Put me where?" Then Mr. Tappitt looked at his wife with a look that was intended to annihilate her, for the time being,—seeing that no words that he could speak had any such effect,—and he hurried out of the room without staying to wash his hands or brush his hair before he went off to preside at the meeting.

Mrs. Tappitt remained where she was for about half an hour and then descended among her daughters.

"Isn't papa going to dine at home?" said Augusta.

"No, my dear; your papa is going to dine with some friends of Mr. Hart's, the candidate who was beaten."

"And has he settled anything about the brewery?" Cherry asked.

"No; not as yet. Your papa is very much troubled about it, and I fear he is not very well. I suppose he must go to this electioneering dinner. When gentlemen take up that sort of thing, they must go on with it. And as they wish your father to preside over the petition, I suppose he he can't very well help himself."

"Is papa going to preside over the petition?" asked Augusta.

"Yes, my dear."

"I hope it won't cost him anything," said Martha. "People say that those petitions do cost a great deal of money."

"It's a very anxious time for me, girls; of course, you must all of you see that. I'm sure when we had our party I didn't think things were going to be as anxious as this, or I wouldn't have had a penny spent in such a way as that. If your papa could bring himself to give up the brewery, everything would be well."

"I do so wish he would," said Cherry, "and let us all go and live at Torquay. I do so hate this nasty dirty old place."

"I shall never live in a house I like so well," said Martha.

"The house is well enough, my dears, and so is the brewery, but it can't be expected that your father should go on working for ever as he does at present. It's too much for his strength;—a great deal too much. I can see it, though I don't suppose any one else can. No one knows, only me, what your father has gone through in that brewery."

"But why doesn't he take Mr. Rowan's offer?" said Cherry.

"Everybody seems to say now that Rowan is ever so rich," said Augusta.

"I suppose papa doesn't like the feeling of being turned out," said Martha.

"He wouldn't be turned out, my dear; not the least in the world," said Mrs. Tappitt. "I don't choose to interfere much myself because, perhaps, I don't understand it; but certainly I should like your papa to retire. I have told him so; but gentlemen sometimes don't like to be told of things."

Mrs. Tappitt could be very severe to her husband, could say to him terrible words if her spirit were put up, as she herself was wont to say.

But she understood that it did not become her to speak ill of their father before her girls. Nor would she willingly have been heard by the servants to scold their master. And though she said terrible things she said them with a conviction that they would not have any terrible effect. Tappitt would only take them for what they were worth, and would measure them by the standard which his old experience had taught him to adopt. When a man has been long consuming red pepper, it takes much red pepper to stimulate his palate. Had Mrs. Tappitt merely advised her husband, in proper conjugal phraseology, to relinquish his trade and to retire to Torquay, her advice, she knew, would have had no weight. She was eager on the subject, feeling convinced that this plan of retirement was for the good of the family generally, and therefore she had advocated it with energy. There may be those who think that a wife goes too far in threatening a husband with a commission of lunacy, and frightening him with a prospect of various fatal diseases; but the dose must be adapted to the constitution, and the palate that is accustomed to large quantities of red pepper must have quantities larger than usual whenever some special culinary effect is to be achieved. On the present occasion Mrs. Tappitt went on talking to the girls of their father in language that was quite eulogistic. No threat against the absent brewer passed her mouth,—or theirs. But they all understood each other, and were agreed that everything was to be done to induce papa to accept Mr. Rowan's offer.

"Then," said Cherry, "he'll marry Rachel Ray, and she'll be mistress of the brewery house."

"Never!" said Mrs. Tappitt, very solemnly. "Never! He'll never be such a fool as that."

"Never!" said Augusta. "Never!"

In the mean time the meeting went on at the Dragon. I can't say that Mr. Tappitt was on this occasion called upon to preside over the petition. He was simply invited to take the chair at a meeting of a dozen men at Baslehurst who were brought together by Mr. Sharpit in order that they might be induced by him to recommend Mr. Hart to employ him, Mr. Sharpit, in getting up the petition in question; and in order that there might be some sufficient temptation to these twelve men to gather themselves together, the dinner at the Dragon was added to the meeting. Mr. Tappitt took the chair in the big, uncarpeted, fusty room upstairs, in which masonic meetings were held once a month, and in which the farmers of the neighbourhood dined once a week, on market days. He took the chair and some seven or eight of his townsmen clustered round him. The others had sent word that they would manage to come in time for the dinner. Mr. Sharpit, before he put the brewer in his place of authority, prompted him as to what he was to do, and in the course of a quarter of an hour two resolutions, already prepared by Mr. Sharpit, had been passed unanimously. Mr. Hart was to be told by the assembled people of Baslehurst that he would certainly be seated by a scrutiny, and he was to be advised to commence his proceedings at once. These resolutions were duly committed to paper by one of Mr. Sharpit's clerks, and Mr. Tappitt, before he sat down to dinner, signed a letter to Mr. Hart on behalf of the electors of Baslehurst. When the work of the meeting was completed it still wanted half an hour to dinner, during which the nine electors of Baslehurst sauntered about the yard of the inn, looked into the stables, talked to the landlady at the bar, indulged themselves with gin and bitters, and found the time very heavy on their hands. They were nine decent-looking, middle-aged men, dressed in black not of the newest, in swallow-tailed coats and black trousers, with chimney-pot hats, and red faces; and as they pottered about the premises of the Dragon they seemed to be very little at their ease.

"What's up, Jim?" said one of the postboys to the ostler.

"Sharpit's got 'em all here to get some more money out of that ere Jew gent;—that's about the ticket," said the ostler.

"He's a clever un," said the postboy.

At last the dinner was ready; and the total number of the party having now completed itself, the liberal electors of Baslehurst prepared to enjoy themselves. No bargain had been made on the subject, but it was understood by them all that they would not be asked to pay for their dinner. Sharpit would see to that. He would probably know how to put it into his little bill; and if he failed in that the risk was his own.

But while the body of the liberal electors was peeping into the stables and drinking gin and bitters, Mr. Sharpit and Mr. Tappitt were engaged in a private conference.

"If you come to me," said Sharpit, "of course I must take it up. The etiquette of the profession don't allow me to decline."

"But why should you wish to decline?" said Tappitt, not altogether pleased by Mr. Sharpit's manner.

"Oh, by no means; no. It's just the sort of work I like;—not much to be made by it, but there's injury to be redressed and justice to be done. Only you see poor Honyman hasn't got much of a practice left to him, and I don't want to take his bread out of his mouth."

"But I'm not to be ruined because of that!"

"As I said before, if you bring the business to me I must take it up. I can't help myself, if I would. And if I do take it up I'll see you through it. Everybody who knows me knows that of me."

"I suppose I shall find you at home about ten to-morrow?"

"Yes; I'll be in my office at ten;—only you should think it well over, you know, Mr. Tappitt. I've nothing to say against Mr. Honyman,—not a word. You'll remember that, if you please, if there should be anything about it afterwards. Ah! you're wanted for the chair, Mr. Tappitt. I'll come and sit alongside of you, if you'll allow me."

The dinner itself was decidedly bad, and the company undoubtedly dull. I am inclined to think that every individual there would have dined more comfortably at home. A horrid mess concocted of old gravy, catsup, and bad wine was distributed under the name of soup. Then there came upon the table half a huge hake,—the very worst fish that swims, a fish with which Devonshire is peculiarly invested. Some hard dark brown mysterious balls were handed round, which on being opened with a knife were found to contain sausage-meat, very greasy and by no means cooked through. Even the *dura ilia* of the liberal electors of Baslehurst declined to make acquaintance with these dainties. After that came the dinner, consisting of a piece of roast beef very raw, and a leg of parboiled mutton, absolutely blue in its state of rawness. When the gory mess was seen which displayed itself on the first incision made into these lumps of meat, the vice-president and one or two of his friends spoke out aloud. That hard and greasy sausage-meat might have been all right for anything they knew to the contrary, and the soup they had swallowed without complaint. But they did know what should be the state of a joint of meat when brought to the table, and therefore they spoke out in their anger. Tappitt himself said nothing that was intended to be carried beyond the waiter, seeing that beer from his own brewery was consumed in the tap of the Dragon; but the vice-president was a hardware dealer with whom the Dragon had but small connection of trade, and he sent terrible messages down to the landlady, threatening her with the Blue Boar, the Mitre, and even with that nasty little pothouse the Chequers. "What is it they expects for their three-and-sixpence?" said the landlady, in her wrath; for it must be understood that Sharpit knew well that he was dealing with one who understood the value of money, and that he did not feel quite sure of passing the dinner in Mr. Hart's bill. Then came a pie with crust an inch thick, which nobody could eat, and a cabinet pudding, so called, full of lumps of suet. I venture to assert that each liberal elector there would have got a better dinner at home, and would have been served with greater comfort; but a public dinner at an inn is the recognized relaxation of a middle-class Englishman in the provinces.

Did he not attend such banquets his neighbours would conceive him to be constrained by domestic tyranny. Others go to them, and therefore he goes also. He is bored frightfully by every speech to which he listens. He is driven to the lowest depths of dismay by every speech which he is called upon to make. He is thoroughly disgusted when he is called on to make no speech. He has no point of sympathy with the neighbours between whom he sits. The wine is bad. The hot water is brought to him cold. His seat is hard and crowded. No attempt is made at the pleasures of conversation. He is continually called upon to stand up that he may pretend to drink a toast in honour of some person or institution for which he cares nothing; for the hero of the evening, as to whom he is probably indifferent; for the church, which perhaps he never enters; the army, which he regards as a hotbed of aristocratic insolence; or for the Queen, whom he reveres and loves by reason of his nature as an Englishman, but against whose fulsome praises as repeated to him ad nauseam in the chairman's speech his very soul unconsciously revolts. It is all a bore, trouble, ennui, nastiness, and discomfort. But yet he goes again and again,—because it is the relaxation natural to an Englishman. The Frenchman who sits for three hours tilted on the hind legs of a little chair with his back against the window-sill of the café, with first a cup of coffee before him and then a glass of sugar and water, is perhaps as much to be pitied as regards his immediate misery; but the liquids which he imbibes are not so injurious to him.

Mr. Tappitt with the eleven other liberal electors of Baslehurst went through the ceremony of their dinner in the usual way. They drank the health of the Queen, and of the volunteers of the county because there was present a podgy little grocer who had enrolled himself in the corps and who was thus enabled to make a speech; and then they drank the health of Mr. Hart, whose ultimate return for the borough they pledged themselves to effect. Having done so much for business, and having thus brought to a conclusion the political work of the evening, they adjourned their meeting to a cosy little parlour near the bar, and then they began to be happy. Some few of the number, including the angry vice-president, who sold hardware, took themselves home to their wives. "Mrs. Tongs keeps him sharp enough by the ears," said Sharpit, winking to Tappitt. "Come along, old fellow, and we'll get a drop of something really hot." Tappitt winked back again and shook his head with an affected laugh; but as he did so he thought of Mrs. T. at home, and the terrible words she had spoken to him;—and at the same moment an idea came across him that Mr. Sharpit was a very dangerous companion.

About half a dozen entered the cosy little parlour, and there they remained for a couple of hours. While sitting in that cosy little parlour they really did enjoy themselves. About nine o'clock they had a bit of the raw beef broiled, and in that guise it was pleasant enough; and the water was hot, and the tobacco was grateful and the stiffness of the evening was gone. The men chatted together and made no more speeches, and they talked of matters which bore a true interest to them. Sharpit explained to them how each man might be assisted in his own business if this rich London tailor could be brought in for the borough. And by degrees they came round to the affairs of the brewery, and Tappitt, as the brandy warmed him, spoke loudly against Rowan.

"By George!" said the podgy grocer, "if anybody would offer me a thousand a year to give up, I'd take it hopping."

"Then I wouldn't," said Tappitt, "and what's more, I won't. But brewing ain't like other businesses;—there's more in it than in most others."

"Of course there is," said Sharpit; "it isn't like any common trade."

"That's true too," said the podgy grocer.

A man usually receives some compensation for having gone through the penance of the chairman's duties. For the remainder of the evening he is entitled to the flattery of his companions, and generally receives it till they become tipsy and insubordinate. Tappitt had not the character of an intemperate man, but on this occasion he did exceed the bounds of a becoming moderation. The room was hot and the tobacco smoke was thick. The wine had been bad and the brandy was strong. Sharpit, too, urged him to new mixtures and stronger denunciations against Rowan, till at last, at eleven o'clock, when he took himself to the brewery, he was not in a condition proper for the father of such daughters or for the husband of such a wife.

"Shall I see him home?" said the podgy grocer to Mr. Sharpit.

Tappitt, with the suspicious quickness of a drunken man, turned sharply upon the podgy and abashed grocer, and abused him for his insolence. He then made his way out of the inn-yard, and along the High Street, and down Brewery Lane to his own door, knowing the way as well as though he had been sober, and passing over it as quickly. Nor did he fall or even stumble, though now and again he reeled slightly. And as he went the idea came strongly upon him that Sharpit was a dangerous man, and that perhaps at this very moment he, Tappitt, was standing on the brink of a precipice. Then he remembered that his wife would surely be watching for him, and as he made his first attempt to insert the latch-key into the door his heart became forgetful of the brandy, and sank low within his breast.

How affairs went between him and Mrs. Tappitt on that night I will not attempt to describe. That she used her power with generosity I do not doubt. That she used it with discretion I am quite convinced. On the following morning at ten o'clock Tappitt was still in bed; but a note had been written by Mrs. T. to Messrs. Sharpit and Longfite, saying that the projected visit had, under altered circumstances, become unnecessary. That Tappitt's head was racked with pain, and his stomach disturbed with sickness, there can be no doubt, and as little that Mrs. T. used the consequent weakness of her husband for purposes of feminine dominion; but this she did with discretion and even with kindness. Only a word or two was said as to the state in which he had returned home,—a word or two with the simple object of putting that dominion on a firm basis. After that Mrs. Tappitt took his condition as an established fact, administered to him the comforts of her medicine-chest and teapot, excused his illness to the girls as having been produced by the fish, and never left his bedside till she had achieved her purpose. If ever a man got tipsy to his own advantage, Mr. Tappitt did so on that occasion. And if ever a man in that condition was treated with forbearing kindness by his wife, Mr. Tappitt was so treated then.

"Don't disturb yourself, T.," she said; "there's nothing wants doing in the brewery, and if it did what would it signify in comparison with your health? The brewery won't be much to you now, thank goodness; and I'm sure you've had enough of it. Thirty years of such work as that would make any man sick and weak. I'm sure I don't wonder at your being ill;—not the least. The wonder is that you've ever stood up against it so long as you have. If you'll take my advice you'll just turn round and try to sleep for an hour or so."

Tappitt took her advice at any rate, so far that he turned round and closed his eyes. Up to this time he had not given way about the brewery. He had uttered no word of assent. But he was gradually becoming aware that he would have to yield before he would be allowed to put on his clothes. And now, in the base and weak condition of his head and stomach, yielding did not seem to him to be so very bad a thing. After all, the brewery was troublesome, the fight was harassing. Rowan was young and strong, and Mr. Sharpit was very dangerous. Rowan, too, had risen in his estimation as in that of others, and he could not longer argue, even to himself, that the stipulated income would not be paid. He did not sleep, but got into that half-drowsy state in which men think of their existing affairs, but without any power of active thought. He knew that he ought to be in his counting-house and at work. He half feared that the world was falling away from him because he was not there. He was ashamed of himself, and sometimes almost entertained a thought of rising up and shaking off his lethargy. But his stomach was bad, and he could not bring himself to move. His head was tormented, and his pillow was soft; and therefore there he lay. He wondered what was the time of day, but did not think of looking at his watch which was under his head. He heard his wife's steps about the room as she shaded some window from his eyes, or crept to the door to give some household order to one of her girls outside; but he did not speak to her, nor she to him. She did not speak to him as long as he lay there motionless, and when he moved with a small low groan she merely offered him some beef tea.

It was nearly six o'clock, and the hour of dinner at the brewery was long passed, when Mrs. Tappitt sat herself down by the bedside determined to reap the fruit of her victory. He had just raised himself in his bed and announced his intention of getting up, — declaring, as he did so, that he would never again eat any of that accursed fish. The moment of his renovation had come upon him, and Mrs. Tappitt perceived that if he escaped from her now, there might even yet be more trouble.

"It wasn't only the fish, T.," she said, with somewhat of sternness in her eye.

"I hardly drank anything," said Tappitt.

"Of course I wasn't there to see what you took," said she; "but you were very bad when you came home last night; — very bad indeed. You couldn't have got in at the door only for me."

"That's nonsense."

"But it is quite true. It's a mercy, T., that neither of the girls saw you. Only think! But there'll be nothing more of that kind, I'm sure, when we are out of this horrid place; and it wouldn't have happened now, only for all this trouble."

To this Tappitt made no answer, but he grunted, and again said that he thought he would get up.

"Of course it's settled now, T., that we're to leave this place."

"I don't know that at all."

"Then, T., you ought to know it. Come now; just look at the common sense of the thing. If we don't give up the brewery what are we to do? There isn't a decent respectable person in the town in favour of our staying here, only that rascal Sharpit. You desired me this morning to write and tell him you'd have nothing more to do with him; and so I did." Tappitt had not seen his wife's letter to the lawyer,—had not asked to see it, and now became aware that his only possible supporter might probably have been driven away from him. Sharpit too, though dangerous as an enemy, was ten times more dangerous as a friend!

"Of course you'll take that young man's offer. Shall I sit down and write a line to Honyman, and tell him to come in the morning?"

Tappitt groaned again and again, said that he would get up, but Mrs. T. would not let him out of bed till he had assented to her proposition that Honyman should be again invited to the brewery. He knew well that the battle was gone from him,—had in truth known it through all those half-comatose hours of his bedridden day. But a man, or a nation, when yielding must still resist even in yielding. Tappitt fumed and fussed under the clothes, protesting that his sending for Honyman would be useless. But the letter was written in his name and sent with his knowledge; and it was perfectly understood that that invitation to Honyman signified an unconditional surrender on the part of Mr. Tappitt. One word Mrs. T. said as she allowed her husband to escape from his prison amidst the blankets, one word by which to mark that the thing was done, and one word only. "I suppose we needn't leave the house for about a month or so,—because it would be inconvenient about the furniture."

"Who's to turn you out if you stay for six months?" said Tappitt.

The thing was marked enough then, and Mrs. Tappitt retired in muffled triumph,—retired when she had made all things easy for the simplest ceremony of dressing.

"Just sponge your face, my dear," she said, "and put on your dressing-gown, and come down for half an hour or so."

"I'm all right now," said Tappitt.

"Oh! quite so;—but I wouldn't go to the trouble of much dressing." Then she left him, descended the stairs, and entered the parlour among her daughters. When there she could not abstain from one blast of the trumpet of triumph. "Well, girls," she said, "it's all settled, and we shall be in Torquay now before the winter."

"No!" said Augusta.

"That'll be a great change," said Martha.

"In Torquay before the winter!" said Cherry. "Oh, mamma, how clever you have been!"

"And now your papa is coming down, and you should thank him for what he's doing for you. It's all for your sake that he's doing it."

Mr. Tappitt crept into the room, and when he had taken his seat in his accustomed arm-chair, the girls went up to him and kissed him. Then they thanked him for his proposed kindness in taking them out of the brewery.

"Oh, papa, it is so jolly!" said Cherry.

Mr. Tappitt did not say much in answer to this;—but luckily there was no necessity that he should say anything. It was an occasion on which silence was understood as giving a perfect consent.

CHAPTER XIII
WHAT TOOK PLACE AT BRAGG'S END FARM

When Mrs. Tappitt had settled within her own mind that the brewery should be abandoned to Rowan, she was by no means, therefore, ready to assent that Rachel Ray should become the mistress of the brewery house. "Never," she had exclaimed when Cherry had suggested such a result; "never!" And Augusta had echoed the protestation, "Never, never!" I will not say that she would have allowed her husband to remain in his business in order that she might thus exclude Rachel from such promotion, but she could not bring herself to believe that Luke Rowan would be so fatuous, so ignorant of his own interests, so deluded, as to marry that girl from Bragg's End! It is thus that the Mrs. Tappitts of the world regard other women's daughters when they have undergone any disappointment as to their own. She had no reason for wishing well to Rowan, and would not have cared if he had taken to his bosom a harpy in marriage; but she could not endure to hear of the success of the girl whose attractions had foiled her own little plan. "I don't believe that the man can ever be such a fool as that!" she said again to Augusta, when on the evening of the day following Tappitt's abdication, a rumour reached the brewery that Luke Rowan had been seen walking out upon the Cawston road.

Mr. Honyman, in accordance with his instructions, called at the brewery on that morning, and was received by Mr. Tappitt with a sullen and almost savage submission. Mrs. T. had endeavoured to catch him first, but in that she had failed; she did, however, manage to see the attorney as he came out from her husband.

"It's all settled," said Honyman; "and I'll see Rowan myself before half an hour is over."

"I'm sure it's a great blessing, Mr. Honyman," said the lady,—not on that occasion assuming any of the glory to herself.

"It was the only thing for him," said Mr. Honyman;—"that is if he didn't like to take the young man in as acting partner."

"That wouldn't have done at all," said Mrs. T. And then the lawyer went his way.

In the mean time Tappitt sat sullen and wretched in the counting-house. Such moments occur in the lives of most of us,—moments in which the real work of life is brought to an end,—and they cannot but be sad. It is very well to talk of ease and dignity; but ease of spirit comes from action only, and the world's dignity is given to those who do the world's work. Let no man put his neck from out of the collar till in truth he can no longer draw the weight attached to it. Tappitt had now got rid of his collar, and he sat very wretched in his brewery counting-house.

"Be I to go, sir?"

Tappitt in his meditation was interrupted by these words, spoken not in a rough voice, and looking up he saw Worts standing in the counting-house before him. Worts had voted for Butler Cornbury, whereas, had he voted for Mr. Hart, Mr. Hart would have been returned; and, upon that, Worts, as a rebellious subject, had received notice to quit the premises. Now his time was out, and he came to ask whether he was to leave the scene of his forty years of work. But what would be the use of sending Worts away even if the wish to punish his contumacy still remained? In another week Worts would be brought back again in triumph, and would tread those brewery floors with the step almost of a master, while he, Tappitt, could tread them only as a stranger, if he were allowed to tread them at all.

"You can stay if you like," said Tappitt, hardly looking up at the man.

"I know you be a going, Mr. Tappitt," said the man; "and I hear you be a going very handsome like. Gentlefolk such as yeu needn't go on working allays like uz. If so be yeu be a going, Mr. Tappitt, I hope yeu and me'll part friendly. We've been together a sight o' years;—too great a sight for uz to part unfriendly."

Mr. Tappitt admitted the argument, shook hands with the man, and then of course took him into his immediate confidence with more warmth than he would have done had there been no quarrel between them. And I think he found some comfort in this. He walked about the premises with Worts, telling him much that was true, and some few things that were not strictly accurate. For instance, he said that he had made up his mind to leave the place, whereas that action of decisive resolution which we call making up our minds had perhaps been done by Mrs. Tappitt rather than by him. But Worts took all these assertions with an air of absolute belief which comforted the brewer. Worts was very wise in his discretion on that day, and threw much oil on the troubled waters; so that Tappitt when he left him bade God bless him, and expressed a hope that the old place might still thrive for his sake.

"And for your'n too, master," said Worts, "for yeu'll allays have the best egg still. The young master, he'll only be a working for yeu."

There was comfort in this thought; and Tappitt, when he went into his dinner, was able to carry himself like a man.

The tidings which had reached Mrs. Tappitt as to Rowan having been seen on that evening walking on the Cawston road with his face towards Bragg's End were true. On that morning Mr. Honyman had come to him, and his career in life was at once settled for him.

"Mr. Tappitt is quite in time, Mr. Honyman," he had said. "But he would not have been in time this day week unless he had consented to pay for what work had been already done; for I had determined to begin at once."

"The truth is, Mr. Rowan, you step into an uncommon good thing; but Mr. Tappitt is tired of the work, and glad to give it up."

Thus the matter was arranged between them, and before nightfall everybody in Baslehurst knew that Tappitt and Rowan had come to terms, and that Tappitt was to retire upon a pension. There was some little discrepancy as to the amount of Tappitt's annuity, the liberal faction asserting that he was to receive two thousand a year, and those of the other side cutting him down to two hundred.

On the evening of that day—in the cool of the evening—Luke Rowan sauntered down the High Street of Baslehurst, and crossed over Cawston bridge. On the bridge he was all alone, and he stood there for a moment or two leaning upon the parapet looking down upon the little stream beneath the arch. During the day many things had occupied him, and he had hardly as yet made up his mind definitely as to what he would do and what he would say during the hours of the evening. From the moment in which Honyman had announced to him Tappitt's intended resignation he became aware that he certainly should go out to Bragg's End before that day was over. It had been with him a settled thing, a thing settled almost without thought ever since the receipt of Rachel's letter, that he would take this walk to Bragg's End when he should have put his affairs at Baslehurst on some stable footing; but that he would not take that walk before he had so done.

"They say," Rachel had written in her letter, "they say that as the business here about the brewery is so very unsettled, they think it probable that you will not have to come back to Baslehurst any more."

In that had been the offence. They had doubted his stability, and, beyond that, had almost doubted his honesty. He would punish them by taking them at their word till both should be put beyond all question. He knew well that the punishment would fall on Rachel, whereas none of the sin would have been Rachel's sin; but he would not allow himself to be deterred by that consideration.

"It is her letter," he said to himself, "and in that way will I answer her. When I do go there again they will all understand me better."

It had been, too, a matter of pride to him that Mr. Comfort and Mrs. Butler Cornbury should thus be made to understand him. He would say nothing of himself and his own purposes to any of them. He would speak neither of his own means nor his own stedfastness. But he would prove to them that he was stedfast, and that he had boasted of nothing which he did not possess. When Mrs. Butler Cornbury had spoken to him down by the Cleeves, asking him of his purpose, and struggling to do a kind thing by Rachel, he had resolved at once that he would tell her nothing. She should find him out. He liked her for loving Rachel; but neither to her, nor even to Rachel herself, would he say more till he could show them that the business about the brewery was no longer unsettled.

But up to this moment—this moment in which he was standing on the bridge, he had not determined what he would say to Rachel or to Rachel's mother. He had never relaxed in his purpose of making Rachel his wife since his first visit to the cottage. He was one who, having a fixed resolve, feels certain of their ultimate success in achieving it. He was now going to Bragg's End to claim that which he regarded as his own; but he had not as yet told himself in what terms he would put forward his claim. So he stood upon the bridge thinking.

He stood upon the bridge thinking, but his thoughts would only go backwards, and would do nothing for him as to his future conduct. He remembered his first walk with her, and the churchyard elms with the setting sun, and the hot dances in Mrs. Tappitt's house; and he remembered them without much of the triumph of a successful lover. It had been very sweet, but very easy. In so saying to himself he by no means threw blame upon Rachel. Things were easy, he thought, and it was almost a pity that they should be so. As for Rachel, nothing could have been more honest or more to his taste, than her mode of learning to love him. A girl who, while intending to accept him, could yet have feigned indifference, would have disgusted him at once. Nevertheless he could not but wish that there had been some castles for him to storm in his career. Tappitt had made but poor pretence of fighting before he surrendered; and as to Rachel, it had not been in Rachel's nature to make any pretence. He passed from the bridge at last without determining what he would say when he reached the cottage, but he did not pass on till he had been seen by the scrutinizing eyes of Miss Pucker.

"If there ain't young Rowan going out to Bragg's End again!" she said to herself, comforting herself, I fear, or striving to comfort herself, with an inward assertion that he was not going there for any good. Striving to comfort herself, but not effectually; for though the assertion was made by herself to herself, yet it was not believed. Though she declared, with well-pronounced mental words, that Luke Rowan was going on that path for no good purpose, she felt a wretched conviction at her heart's core that Rachel Ray would be made to triumph over her and her early suspicions by a happy marriage. Nevertheless she carried the tidings up into Baslehurst, and as she repeated it to the grocer's daughters and the baker's wife she shook her head with as much apparent satisfaction as though she really believed that Rachel oscillated between a ruined name and a broken heart.

He walked on very slowly towards Bragg's End, as though he almost dreaded the interview, swinging his stick as was his custom, and keeping his feet on the grassy edges of the road till he came to the turn which brought him on to the green. When on the green he did not take the highway, but skirted along under Farmer Sturt's hedge, so that he had to pass by the entrance of the farmyard before he crossed over to the cottage. Here, just inside her own gate, he encountered Mrs. Sturt standing alone. She had been intent on the cares of her poultry-yard till she had espied Luke Rowan; but then she had forgotten chickens and ducks and all, and had given herself up to thoughts of Rachel's happiness in having her lover back again.

"It's he as sure as eggs," she had said to herself when she first saw him; "how mortal slow he do walk, to be sure! If he was coming as joe to me I'd soon shake him into quicker steps than them."

"Oh, Mrs. Sturt!" said he, "I hope you're quite well," and he stopped short at her gate.

"Pretty bobbish, thankee, Mr. Rowan; and how's yourself? Are you going over to the cottage this evening?"

"Who's at home there, Mrs. Sturt?"

"Well, they're all at home; Mrs. Ray, and Rachel, and Mrs. Prime. I doubt whether you know the eldest daughter, Mr. Rowan?"

Luke did not know Mrs. Prime, and by no means wished to spend any of the hours of the present evening in making her acquaintance.

"Is Mrs. Prime there?" he asked.

"'Deed she is, Mr. Rowan. She's come back these last two days."

Thereupon Rowan paused for a moment, having carefully placed himself inside the gate-posts of the farmyard so that he might not be seen by the inmates of the cottage, if haply he had hitherto escaped their eyes.

"Mrs. Sturt," said he, "I wonder whether you'd do me a great favour."

"That depends—" said Mrs. Sturt. "If it's to do any good to any of them over there, I will."

"If I wanted to do harm to any of them I shouldn't come to you."

"Well, I should hope not. Is she and you going to be one, Mr. Rowan? That's about the whole of it."

"It shan't be my fault if we're not," said Rowan.

"That's spoken honest," said the lady; "and now I'll do anything in my power to bring you together. If you'll just go into my little parlour, I'll bring her to you in five seconds; I will indeed, Mr. Rowan. You won't mind going through the kitchen for once, will you?"

Luke did not mind going through the kitchen, and immediately found himself shut up in Mrs. Sturt's back parlour, looking out among the mingled roses and cabbages.

Mrs. Sturt walked quickly across the road to the cottage door, and went at once to the open window of the sitting-room. Mrs. Ray was there with a book in her hand,—a serious book, the perusal of which I fear was in some degree due to the presence of her elder daughter; and Mrs. Prime was there with another book, evidently very serious; and Rachel was there too, seated on the sofa, deeply buried in the manipulation of a dress belonging to her mother. Mrs. Sturt was sure at once that they had not seen Luke Rowan as he passed inside the farmyard gate, and that they did not suspect that he was near them.

"Oh, Mrs. Sturt, is that you?" said the widow, looking up. "You'll just come in for a minute, won't you?" and Mrs. Ray showed by a suppressed yawn that her attention had not been deeply fixed by that serious book. Rachel looked up, and bade the visitor welcome with a little nod; but it was not a cheery nod as it would have been in old days, before her sorrow had come upon her.

"I'll have the cherries back in her cheeks before the evening's over," said Mrs. Sturt to herself, as she looked at the pale-faced girl. Mrs. Prime also made some little salutation to their neighbour; but she did so with the very smallest expenditure of thoughts or moments. Mrs. Sturt was all very well, but Mrs. Prime had greater work on hand than gossiping with Mrs. Sturt.

"I'll not just come in, thankee, Mrs. Ray; but if it ain't troubling you I want to speak a word to you outside; and a word to Rachel too, if she don't mind coming."

"A word to me!" said Rachel getting up and putting down her dress. Her thoughts now-a-days were always fixed on the same subject, and it seemed that any special word to her must have reference to that. Mrs. Ray also got up, leaving her mark in her book. Mrs. Prime went on reading, harder than ever. There was to be some conference of importance from which she could not but feel herself to be excluded in a very special way. Something wicked was surely to be proposed, or she would have been allowed to hear it. She said nothing, but her head was almost shaken by the vehemence with which she read the book in her lap.

Mrs. Sturt retired beyond the precincts of the widow's front garden before she said a word. Rachel had followed her first through the gate, and Mrs. Ray came after with her apron turned over her head. "What is it, Mrs. Sturt?" said Rachel. "Have you heard anything?"

"Heard anything? Well; I'm always a hearing of something. Do you slip across the green while I speak just one word to your mother. And Rachel, wait for me at the gate. Mrs. Ray, he's in my little parlour."

"Who? not Luke Rowan?"

"But he is though; that very young man! He's come over to make it up with her. He's told me so with his own mouth. You may be as sure of it as, — as, — as anything. You leave 'em to me, Mrs. Ray; I wouldn't bring them together if it wasn't for good. It's my belief our pet would a' died if he hadn't come back to her — it is then." And Mrs. Sturt put her apron up to her eyes.

Rachel having paused for a moment, as she looked first at her mother and then at Mrs. Sturt, had done as she was bidden, and had walked quickly across the green. Mrs. Ray, when she heard her neighbour's tidings, stood fixed by dismay and dread, mingled with joy. She had longed for his coming back; but now that he was there, close upon them, intending to do all that she had wished him to do, she was half afraid of him! After all was he not a young man; and might he not, even yet, be a wolf? She was horrorstricken at the idea of sending Rachel over to see a lover, and looked back at the cottage window, towards Mrs. Prime, as though to see whether she was being watched in her iniquity. "Oh, Mrs. Sturt!" she said, "why didn't you give us time to think about it?"

"Give you time! How could I give you time, and he here on the spot? There's been too much time to my thinking. When young folk are agreeable and the old folk are agreeable too, there can't be too little time. Come along over and we'll talk of it in the kitchen while they talks in the parlour. He'd a' been in there among you all only for Mrs. Prime. She is so dour like for a young man to have to say anything before her, of the likes of that. That's why I took him into our place."

They overtook Rachel at the house door and they all went through together into the great kitchen. "Oh, Rachel!" said Mrs. Ray. "Oh, dear!"

"What is it, mamma?" said Rachel. Then looking into her mother's face, she guessed the truth. "Mamma," she said, "he's here! Mr. Rowan is here!" And she took hold of her mother's arm, as though to support herself.

"And that's just the truth," said Mrs. Sturt, triumphantly. "He's through there in the little parlour, and you must just go to him, my dear, and hear what he's got to say to you."

"Oh, mamma!" said Rachel.

"I suppose you must do what she tells you," said Mrs. Ray.

"Of course she must," said Mrs. Sturt.

"Mamma, you must go to him," said Rachel.

"That won't do at all," said Mrs. Sturt.

"And why has he come here?" said Rachel.

"Ah! I wonder why," said Mrs. Sturt. "I wonder why any young man should come on such an errand! But it won't do to leave him there standing in my parlour by himself, so do you come along with me."

So saying Mrs. Sturt took Rachel by the arm to lead her away. Mrs. Ray in this great emergency was perfectly helpless. She could simply look at her daughter with imploring, loving eyes, and stand quivering in doubt against the dresser. Mrs. Sturt had very decided views on the matter. She had put Luke Rowan into the parlour with a promise that she would bring Rachel to him there, and she was not going to break her word through any mock delicacy. The two young people liked one another, and they should have this opportunity of saying so in each other's hearing. So she took Rachel by the arm, and opening the door of the parlour led her into the room. "Mr. Rowan," she said, "when you and Miss Rachel have had your say out, you'll find me and her mamma in the kitchen." Then she closed the door and left them alone.

Rachel, when first summoned out of the cottage, had felt at once that Mrs. Sturt's visit must have reference to Luke Rowan. Indeed everything with her in her present moods had some reference to him,—some reference though it might be ever so remote. But now before she had time to form a thought, she was told that he was there in the same house with her, and that she was taken to him in order that she might hear his words and speak her own. It was very sudden; and for the space of a few moments she would have fled away from Mrs. Sturt's kitchen had such flight been possible. Since Rowan had gone from her there had been times in which she would have fled to him, in which she would have journeyed alone any distance so that she might tell him of her love, and ask whether she had got any right to hope for his. But all that seemed to be changed. Though her mother was there with her and her friend, she feared that this seeking of her lover was hardly maidenly. Should he not have come to her,—every foot of the way to her feet, and there have spoken if he had aught to say, before she had been called on to make any sign? Would he like her for thus going to him? But then she had no chance of escape. She found herself in Mrs. Sturt's kitchen under her mother's sanction, before she had been able to form any purpose; and then an idea did come to her, even at that moment, that poor Luke would have had a hard task of it in her sister's presence. When she was first told that he was there in the farm-house parlour, her courage left her and she dreaded the encounter; but she was able to collect her thoughts as she passed out of the kitchen, and across the passage, and when she followed Mrs. Sturt into the room she had again acquired the power to carry herself as a woman having a soul of her own.

"Rachel!" Rowan said, stepping up to her and tendering his hand to her. "I have come to answer your letter in person."

"I knew," she said, "when I wrote it, that my letter did not deserve any answer. I did not expect an answer."

"But am I wrong now to bring you one in person? I have thought so much of seeing you again! Will you not say a word of welcome to me?"

"I am glad to see you, Mr. Rowan."

"Mr. Rowan! Nay; if it is to be Mr. Rowan I may as well go back to Baslehurst. It has come to that, that it must be Luke now, or there must be no naming of names between us. You chided me once when I called you Rachel."

"You called me so once, sir, when I should have chided you and did not. I remember it well. You were very wrong, and I was very foolish."

"But I may call you Rachel now?" Then, when she did not answer him at the moment, he asked the question again in that imperious way which was common with him. "May I not call you now as I please? If it be not so my coming here is useless. Come, Rachel, say one word to me boldly. Do you love me well enough to be my wife?"

She was standing at the open window, looking away from him, while he remained at a little distance from her as though he would not come close to her till he had exacted from her some positive assurance of her love as a penance for the fault committed by her letter. He certainly was not a soft lover, nor by any means inclined to abate his own privileges. He paused a moment as though he thought that his last question must elicit a plain reply. But no reply to it came. She still looked away from him through the window, as though resolved that she would not speak till his mood should have become more tender.

"You said something in your letter," he continued, "about my affairs here in Baslehurst being unsettled. I would not show myself here again till that matter was arranged."

"It was not I," she said, turning sharply round upon him. "It was not I who thought that."

"It was in your letter, Rachel."

"Do you know so little of a girl like me as to suppose that what was written there came from me, myself? Did I not tell you that I said what I was told to say? Did I not explain to you that mamma had gone to Mr. Comfort? Did you not know that all that had come from him?"

"I only know that I read it in your letter to me,—the only letter you had ever written to me."

"You are unfair to me, Mr. Rowan. You know that you are unfair."

"Call me Luke," he said. "Call me by my own name."

"Luke," she said, "you are unfair to me."

"Then by heavens it shall be for the last time. May things in this world and the next go well with me as I am fair to you for the future!" So saying he came up close to her, and took her at once in his arms.

"Luke, Luke; don't. You frighten me; indeed you do."

"You shall give me a fair open kiss, honestly, before I leave you,—in truth you shall. If you love me, and wish to be my wife, and intend me to understand that you and I are now pledged to each other beyond the power of any person to separate us by his advice, or any mother by her fears, give me a bold, honest kiss, and I will understand that it means all that."

Still she hesitated for a moment, turning her face away from him while he held her by the waist. She hesitated while she was weighing the meaning of his words, and taking them home to herself as her own. Then she turned her neck towards him, still holding back her head till her face was immediately under his own, and after another moment's pause she gave him her pledge as he had asked it. Mrs. Sturt's words had come true, and the cherries had returned to her cheek.

"My own Rachel! And now tell me one thing: are you happy?"

"So happy!"

"My own one!"

"But, Luke,—I have been wretched;—so wretched! I thought you would never come back to me."

"And did that make you wretched?"

"Ah!—did it? What do you think yourself? When I wrote that letter to you I knew I had no right to expect that you would think of me again."

"But how could I help thinking of you when I loved you?"

"And then when mamma saw you in Exeter, and you sent me no word of message!"

"I was determined to send none till this business was finished."

"Ah! that was cruel. But you did not understand. I suppose no man can understand. I couldn't have believed it myself till—till after you had gone away. It seemed as though all the sun had deserted us, and that everything was cold and dark."

They stood at the open window looking out upon the roses and cabbages till the patience of Mrs. Sturt and of Mrs. Ray was exhausted. What they said, beyond so much of their words as I have repeated, need not be told. But when a low half-abashed knock at the door interrupted them, Luke thought that they had hardly been there long enough to settle the preliminaries of the affair which had brought him to Bragg's End.

"May we come in?" said Mrs. Sturt very timidly.

"Oh, mamma, mamma!" said Rachel, and she hid her face upon her mother's shoulder.

CHAPTER XIV
MRS. PRIME READS HER RECANTATION

Above an hour had passed after the interruption mentioned at the end of the last chapter before Mrs. Ray and Rachel crossed back from the farm-house to the cottage, and when they went they went alone. During that hour they had been sitting in Mrs. Sturt's parlour; and when at last they got up to go they did not press Luke Rowan to go with them. Mrs. Prime was at the cottage, and it was necessary that everything should be explained to her before she was asked to give her hand to her future brother-in-law. The farmer had come in and had joked his joke, and Mrs. Sturt had clacked over them as though they were a brood of chickens of her own hatching; and Mrs. Ray had smiled and cried, and sobbed and laughed till she had become almost hysterical. Then she had jumped up from her seat, saying, "Oh, dear, what will Dorothea think has become of us?" After that Rachel insisted upon going, and the mother and daughter returned across the green, leaving Luke at the farm-house, ready to take his departure as soon as Mrs. Ray and Rachel should have safely reached their home.

"I knew thee was minded stedfast to take her," said Mrs. Sturt, "when it came out upon the newspaper how thou hadst told them all in Baslehurst that thou wouldst wed none but a Baslehurst lass."

In answer to this Luke protested that he had not thought of Rachel when he was making that speech, and tried to explain that all that was "soft sawder" as he called it, for the election. But the words were too apposite to the event, and the sentiment too much in accordance with Mrs. Sturt's chivalric views to allow of her admitting the truth of any such assurance as this.

"I know," she said; "I know. And when I read them words in the newspaper I said to the gudeman there, we shall have bridecake from the cottage now before Christmas."

"For the matter of that, so you shall," said Luke, shaking hands with her as he went, "or the fault will not be mine."

Rachel, as she followed her mother out from the farmyard gate, had not a word to say. Could it have been possible she would have wished to remain silent for the remainder of the evening and for the night, so that she might have time to think of this thing which she had done, and to enjoy the full measure of her happiness. Hitherto she had hardly had any joy in her love. The cup had been hardly given to her to drink before it had been again snatched away, and since then she had been left to think that the draught for which she longed would never again be offered to her lips. The whole affair had now been managed so suddenly, and the action had been so quick, that she had hardly found a moment for thought. Could it be that things were so fixed that there was no room for further disappointment? She had been scalded so cruelly that she still feared the hot water. Her heart was sore with the old hurt, as the head that has ached will be still sore when the actual malady has passed away. She longed for hours of absolute quiet, in which she might make herself sure that her malady had also passed away, and that the soreness which remained came only from the memory of former pain. But there was no such perfect rest within her reach as yet.

"Will you tell her or shall I?" said Mrs. Ray, pausing for a moment at the cottage gate.

"You had better tell her, mamma."

"I suppose she won't set herself against it; will she?"

"I hope not, mamma. I shall think her very ill-natured if she does. But it can't make any real difference now, you know."

"No; it can't make any difference. Only it will be so uncomfortable."

Then with half-frightened, muffled steps they entered their own house, and joined Mrs. Prime in the sitting-room.

Mrs. Prime was still reading the serious book; but I am bound to say that her mind had not been wholly intent upon it during the long absence of her mother and sister. She had struggled for a time to ignore the slight fact that her companions were away gossiping with the neighbouring farmer's wife; she had made a hard fight with her book, pinning her eyes down upon the page over and over again, as though in pinning down her eyes she could pin down her mind also. But by degrees the delay became so long that she was tantalized into surmises as to the subject of their conversation. If it were not wicked, why should not she have been allowed to share it? She did not imagine it to be wicked according to the world's ordinary wickedness;—but she feared that it was wicked according to that tone of morals to which she was desirous of tying her mother down as a bond slave. They were away talking about love and pleasure, and those heart-throbbings in which her sister had so unfortunately been allowed to indulge. She felt all but sure that some tidings of Luke Rowan had been brought in Mrs. Sturt's budget of news, and she had never been able to think well of Luke Rowan since the evening on which she had seen him standing with Rachel in the churchyard. She knew nothing against him; but she had then made up her mind that he was pernicious, and she could not bring herself to own that she had been wrong in that opinion. She had been loud and defiant in her denunciation when she had first suspected Rachel of having a lover. Since that she had undergone some troubles of her own by which the tone of her remonstrances had been necessarily moderated; but even now she could not forgive her sister such a lover as Luke Rowan. She would have been quite willing to see her sister married, but the lover should have been dingy, black-coated, lugubrious, having about him some true essence of the tears of the valley of tribulation. Alas, her sister's taste was quite of another kind!

"I'm afraid you will have been thinking that we were never coming back again," said Mrs. Ray, as she entered the room.

"No, mother, I didn't think that. But I thought you were staying late with Mrs. Sturt."

"So we were,—and really I didn't think we had been so long. But, Dorothea, there was some one else over there besides Mrs. Sturt, and he kept us."

"He! What he?" said Mrs. Prime. She had not even suspected that the lover had been over there in person.

"Mr. Rowan, my dear. He has been at the farm."

"What! the young man that was dismissed from Mr. Tappitt's?"

It was ill said of her,—very ill said, and so she was herself aware as soon as the words were out of her mouth. But she could not help it. She had taken a side against Luke Rowan, and could not restrain herself from ill-natured words. Rachel was still standing in the middle of the room when she heard her lover thus described; but she would not condescend to plead in answer to such a charge. The colour came to her cheeks, and she threw up her head with a gesture of angry pride, but at the moment she said nothing. Mrs. Ray spoke.

"It seems to me, Dorothea," she said, "that you are mistaken there. I think he has dismissed Mr. Tappitt."

"I don't know much about it," said Mrs. Prime; "I only know that they've quarrelled."

"But it would be well that you should learn, because I'm sure you will be glad to think as well of your brother-in-law as possible."

"Do you mean that he is engaged to marry Rachel?"

"Yes, Dorothea. I think we may say that it is all settled now;—mayn't we, Rachel? And a very excellent young man he is,—and as for being well off, a great deal better than what a child of mine could have expected. And a fine comely fellow he is, as a woman's eye would wish to rest on."

"Beauty is but skin deep," said Mrs. Prime, with no little indignation in her tone, that a thing so vile as personal comeliness should have been mentioned by her mother on such an occasion.

"When he came out here and drank tea with us that evening," continued Mrs. Ray, "I took a liking to him most unaccountable, unless it was that I had a foreshadowing that he was going to be so near and dear to me."

"Mother, there can have been nothing of the kind. You should not say such things. The Lord in his providence allows us no foreshadowing of that kind."

"At any rate I liked him very much; didn't I, Rachel?—from the first moment I set eyes on him. Only I don't think he'll ever do away with cider in Devonshire, because of the apple trees. But if people are to drink beer it stands to reason that good beer will be better than bad."

All this time Rachel had not spoken a word, nor had her sister uttered anything expressive of congratulation or good wishes. Now, as Mrs. Ray ceased, there came a silence in the room, and it was incumbent on the elder sister to break it.

"If this matter is settled, Rachel—"

"It is settled,—I think," said Rachel.

"If it is settled I hope that it may be for your lasting happiness and eternal welfare."

"I hope it will," said Rachel.

"Marriage is a most important step."

"That's quite true, my dear," said Mrs. Ray.

"A most important step, and one that requires the most exact circumspection,—especially on the part of the young woman. I hope you may have known Mr. Rowan long enough to justify your confidence in him."

It was still the voice of a raven! Mrs. Prime as she spoke thus knew that she was croaking, and would have divested herself of her croak and spoken joyously, had such mode of speech been possible to her. But it was not possible. Though she would permit no such foreshadowings as those at which her mother had hinted, she had committed herself to forebodings against this young man, to such extent that she could not wheel her thoughts round and suddenly think well of him. She could not do so as yet, but she would make the struggle.

"God bless you, Rachel!" she said, when they parted for the night. "You have my best wishes for your happiness. I hope you do not doubt my love because I think more of your welfare in another world than in this." Then she kissed her sister and they parted for the night.

Rachel now shared her mother's room; and from her mother, when they were alone together, she received abundance of that sympathy for which her heart was craving.

"You mustn't mind Dorothea," the widow said.

"No, mamma; I do not."

"I mean that you mustn't mind her seeming to be so hard. She means well through it all, and is as affectionate as any other woman."

"Why did she say that he had been dismissed when she knew that it wasn't true?"

"Ah, my dear! can't you understand? When she first heard of Mr. Rowan—"

"Call him Luke, mamma."

"When she first heard of him she was taught to believe that he was giddy, and that he didn't mean anything."

"Why should she think evil of people? Who taught her?"

"Miss Pucker, and Mr. Prong, and that set."

"Yes; and they are the people who talk most of Christian charity!"

"But, my dear, they don't mean to be uncharitable. They try to do good. If Dorothea really thought that this young man was a dangerous acquaintance what could she do but say so? And you can't expect her to turn round all in a minute. Think how she has been troubled herself about this affair of Mr. Prong's."

"But that's no reason she should say that Luke is dangerous. Dangerous! What makes me so angry is that she should think everybody is a fool except herself. Why should anybody be more dangerous to me than to anybody else?"

"Well, my dear, I think that perhaps she is not so wrong there. Of course everything is all right with you now, and I'm sure I'm the happiest woman in the world to feel that it is so. I don't know how to be thankful enough when I think how things have turned out;—but when I first heard of him I thought he was dangerous too."

"But you don't think he is dangerous now, mamma?"

"No, my dear; of course I don't. And I never did after he drank tea here that night; only Mr. Comfort told me it wouldn't be safe not to see how things went a little before you,—you understand, dearest?"

"Yes, I understand. I ain't a bit obliged to Mr. Comfort, though I mean to forgive him because of Mrs. Cornbury. She has behaved best through it all,—next to you, mamma."

I am afraid it was late before Mrs. Ray went to sleep that night, and I almost doubt whether Rachel slept at all. It seemed to her that in the present condition of her life sleep could hardly be necessary. During the last month past she had envied those who slept while she was kept awake by her sorrow. She had often struggled to sleep as she sat in her chair, so that she might escape for a few moments from the torture of her waking thoughts. But why need she sleep now that every thought was a new pleasure? There was no moment that she had ever passed with him that had not to be recalled. There was no word of his that had not to be re-weighed. She remembered, or fancied that she remembered, her idea of the man when her eye first fell upon his outside form. She would have sworn that her first glance of him had conveyed to her far more than had ever come to her from many a day's casual looking at any other man. She could almost believe that he had been specially made and destined for her behoof. She blushed even while lying in bed as she remembered how the gait of the man, and the tone of his voice, had taken possession of her eyes and ears from the first day on which she had met him. When she had gone to Mrs. Tappitt's party, so consciously alive to the fact that he was to be there, she had told herself that she was sure she thought no more of him than of any other man that she might meet; but she now declared to herself that she had been a weak fool in thus attempting to deceive herself; that she had loved him from the first,—or at any rate from that evening when he had told her of the beauty of the clouds; and that from that day to the present hour there had been no other chance of happiness to her but that chance which had now been so wondrously decided in her favour. When she came down to breakfast on the next morning she was very quiet,—so quiet that her sister almost thought she was frightened at her future prospects; but I think that there was no such fear. She was so happy that she could afford to be tranquil in her happiness.

On that day Rowan came out to the cottage in the evening and was formally introduced to Mrs. Prime. Mrs. Ray, I fear, did not find the little tea-party so agreeable on that evening as she had done on the previous occasion. Mrs. Prime did make some effort at conversation; she did endeavour to receive the young man as her future brother-in-law; she was gracious to him with such graciousness as she possessed;—but the duration of their meal was terribly long, and even Mrs. Ray herself felt relieved when the two lovers went forth together for their evening walk. I think there must have been some triumph in Rachel's heart as she tied on her hat before she started. I think she must have remembered the evening on which her sister had been so urgent with her to go to the Dorcas meeting;—when she had so obstinately refused that invitation, and had instead gone out to meet the Tappitt girls, and had met with them the young man of whom her sister had before been speaking with so much horror. Now he was there on purpose to take her with him, and she went forth with him, leaning lovingly on his arm, while yet close under her sister's eyes. I think there must have been a gleam of triumph in her face as she put her hand with such confidence well round her lover's arm.

Girls do triumph in their lovers,—in their acknowledged and permitted lovers, as young men triumph in their loves which are not acknowledged or perhaps permitted. A man's triumph is for the most part over when he is once allowed to take his place at the family table, as a right, next to his betrothed. He begins to feel himself to be a sacrificial victim,—done up very prettily with blue and white ribbons round his horns, but still an ox prepared for sacrifice. But the girl feels herself to be exalted for those few weeks as a conqueror, and to be carried along in an ovation of which that bucolic victim, tied round with blue ribbons on to his horns, is the chief grace and ornament. In this mood, no doubt, both Rachel and Luke Rowan went forth, leaving the two widows together in the cottage.

"It is pretty to see her so happy, isn't it now?" said Mrs. Ray.

The question for the moment made Mrs. Prime uncomfortable and almost wretched, but it gave her the opportunity which in her heart she desired of recanting her error in regard to Luke Rowan's character. She wished to give in her adhesion to the marriage,—to be known to have acknowledged its fitness so that she could, with some true word of sisterly love, wish her sister well. In Rachel's presence she could not have first made this recantation. Though Rachel spoke no triumph, there was a triumph in her eye, which prevented almost the possibility of such yielding on the part of Dorothea. But when the thing should have been once done, when she should once have owned that Rachel was not wrong, then gradually she could bring herself round to the utterance of some kindly expression.

"Pretty," she said; "yes, it is pretty. I do not know that anybody ever doubted its prettiness."

"And isn't it nice too? Dear girl! It does make me so happy to see her light-hearted again. She has had a sad time of it, Dorothea, since we made her write that letter to him; a very sad time of it."

"People here, mother, do mostly have what you call a sad time of it. Are we not taught that it is better for us that it should be so? Have not you and I, mother, had a sad time of it? It would be all sad enough if this were to be the end of it."

"Yes, just so; of course we know that. But it can't be wrong that she should be happy now, when things are so bright all around her. You wouldn't have thought it better for her, or for him either, that they should be kept apart, seeing that they really love each other?"

"No; I don't say that. If they love one another of course it is right that they should marry. I only wish we had known him longer."

"I am not sure that these things always go much better because young people have known each other all their lives. It seems to be certain that he is an industrious, steady young man. Everybody seems to speak well of him now."

"Well, mother, I have nothing to say against him,—not a word. And if it will give Rachel any pleasure,—though I don't suppose it will, the least in the world; but if it would, she may know that I think she has done wisely to accept him."

"Indeed it will; the greatest pleasure."

"And I hope they will be happy together for very many years. I love Rachel dearly, though I fear she does not think so, and anything I have said, I have said in love, not in anger."

"I'm sure of that, Dorothea."

"Now that she is to be settled in life as a married woman, of course she must not look for counsel either to you or to me. She must obey him, and I hope that God may give him grace to direct her steps aright."

"Amen!" said Mrs. Ray, solemnly. It was thus that Mrs. Prime read her recantation, which was repeated on that evening to Rachel with some little softening touches. "You won't be living together in the same house after a bit," said Mrs. Ray, thinking, with some sadness, that those little evening festivities of buttered toast and thick cream were over for her now,—"but I do hope you will be friends."

"Of course we will, mamma. She has only to put out her hand the least little bit in the world, and I will go the rest of the way. As for her living, I don't know what will be best about that, because Luke says that of course you'll come and live with us."

It was two or three days after this that Rachel saw the Tappitt girls for the first time since the fact of her engagement had become known. It was in the evening, and she had been again walking with Luke, when she met them; but at that moment she was alone. Augusta would have turned boldly away, though they had all come closely together before either had been aware of the presence of the other. But to this both Martha and Cherry objected.

"We have heard of your engagement," said Martha, "and we congratulate you. You have heard, of course, that we are going to move to Torquay, and we hope that you will be comfortable at the brewery."

"Yes," said Augusta, "the place isn't what it used to be, and so we think it best to go. Mamma has already looked at a villa near Torquay, which will suit us delightfully."

Then they passed on, but Cherry remained behind to say another word. "I am so happy," said Cherry, "that you and he have hit it off. He's a charming fellow, and I always said he was to fall in love with you. After the ball of course there wasn't a doubt about it. Mind you send us cake, dear; and by-and-by we'll come and see you at the old place, and be better friends than ever we were."

CHAPTER XV
CONCLUSION

Early in November Mr. Tappitt officially announced his intention of abdicating, and the necessary forms and deeds and parchment obligations were drawn out, signed and sealed, for the giving up of the brewery to Luke Rowan. Mr. Honyman's clerk revelled in thinly-covered folio sheets to the great comfort and profit of his master; while Mr. Sharpit went about Baslehurst declaring that Tappitt was an egregious ass, and hinting that Rowan was little better than a clever swindler. What he said, however, had but little effect on Baslehurst. It had become generally understood that Rowan would spend money in the town, employing labour and struggling to go ahead, and Baslehurst knew that such a man was desirable as a citizen. The parchments were prepared, and the signatures were written with the necessary amount of witnessing, and Tappitt and Rowan once more met each other on friendly terms. Tappitt had endeavoured to avoid this, pleading, both to Honyman and to his wife, that his personal dislike to the young man was as great as ever; but they had not permitted him thus to indulge his wrath. Mr. Honyman pointed out to Mrs. Tappitt that such ill-humour might be very detrimental to their future interests, and Tappitt had been made to give way. We may as well declare at once that the days of Tappitt's domestic dominion were over, as is generally the case with a man who retires from work and allows himself to be placed, as a piece of venerable furniture, in the chimney corner. Hitherto he, and he only, had known what funds could be made available out of the brewery for household purposes; and Mrs. Tappitt had been subject, at every turn of her life, to provoking intimations of reduced profits: but now there was the clear thousand a year, and she could demand her rights in accordance with that sum. Tappitt, too, could never again stray away from home with mysterious hints that matters connected with malt and hops must be discussed at places in which beer was consumed. He had no longer left to him any excuse for deviating from the regular course of his life even by a hair's breadth; and before two years were over he had learned to regard it almost as a favour to be allowed to take a walk with one of his own girls. No man should abdicate,—unless, indeed, he does so for his soul's advantage. As to happiness in this life it is hardly compatible with that diminished respect which ever attends the relinquishing of labour. Otium cum dignitate is a dream. There is no such position at any rate for the man who has once worked. He may have the ease or he may have the dignity; but he can hardly combine the two. This truth the unfortunate Tappitt learned before he had been three months settled in the Torquay villa.

He was called upon to meet Rowan on friendly terms, and he obeyed. The friendship was not very cordial, but such as it was it served its purpose. The meeting took place in the dining-room of the brewery, and Mrs. Tappitt was present on the occasion. The lady received her visitor with some little affectation of grandeur, while T., standing with his hands in his pockets on his own rug, looked like a whipped hound. The right hand he was soon forced to bring forth, as Rowan demanded it that he might shake it.

"I am very glad that this affair has been settled between us amicably," said Luke, while he still held the hand of the abdicating brewer.

"Yes; well, I suppose it's for the best," said Tappitt, bringing out his words uncomfortably and with hesitation. "Take care and mind what you're about, or I suppose I shall have to come back again."

"There'll be no fear of that, I think," said Rowan.

"I hope not," said Mrs. Tappitt, with a tone that showed that she was much better able to master the occasion than her husband. "I hope not; but this is a great undertaking for so young a man, and I trust you feel your responsibility. It would be disagreeable to us, of course, to have to return to the brewery after having settled ourselves pleasantly at Torquay; but we shall have to do so if things go wrong with you."

"Don't be frightened, Mrs. Tappitt; you shall never have to come back here."

"I hope not; but it is always well to be on one's guard. I am sure you must be aware that Mr. Tappitt has behaved to you very generously; and if you have the high principle for which we are willing to give you credit, and which you ought to possess for the management of such an undertaking as the brewery, you will be careful that me and my daughters shan't be put to inconvenience by any delay in paying up the income regularly."

"Don't be afraid about that, Mrs. Tappitt."

"Into the bank on quarter day, if you please, Mr. Rowan. Short accounts make long friends. And as Mr. T. won't want to be troubled with letters and such-like, you can send me a line to Montpellier Villa, Torquay, just to say that it's done."

"Oh, I'll see to that," said Tappitt.

"My dear, as Mr. Rowan is so young for the business there'll be nothing like getting him to write a letter himself, saying that the money is paid. It'll keep him up to the mark like, and I'm sure I shan't mind the trouble."

"Don't you be alarmed about the money, Mrs. Tappitt," said Rowan, laughing; "and in order that you may know how the old shop is going on, I'll always send you at Christmas sixteen gallons of the best stuff we're brewing."

"That will be a very proper little attention, Mr. Rowan, and we shall be happy to drink success to the establishment. Here's some cake and wine on the table, and perhaps you'll do us the favour to take a glass, — so as to bury any past unkindness. T., my love, will you pour out the wine?"

It was twelve o'clock in the day, and the port wine, which had been standing for the last week in its decanter, was sipped by Luke Rowan without any great relish. But it also served its purpose, — and the burial service over past unkindness was performed with as much heartiness as the nature of the entertainment admitted. It was not as yet full four months since Rowan had filled Rachel's glass with champagne in that same room. Then he had made himself quite at home in the house as a member of Mr. Tappitt's family; but now he was going to be at home there as master of the establishment. As he put down the glass he could not help looking round the room, and suggesting to himself the changes he would make. As seen at present, the parlour of the brewery was certainly a dull room. It was very long since the wainscoting had been painted, longer since the curtains or carpets had been renewed. It was dark and dingy. But then so were the Tappitts themselves. Before Rachel should be brought there he would make the place as bright as herself.

They said to him no word about his marriage. As for Tappitt he said few words about anything; and Mrs. Tappitt, with all her wish to be gracious, could not bring herself to mention Rachel Ray. Even between her and her daughters there was no longer any utterance of Rachel's name. She had once declared to Augusta, with irrepressible energy, that the man was a greater fool than she had ever believed possible, but after that it had been felt that the calamity would be best endured in silence.

When that interview in the dining-room was over, Rowan saw no more of Mrs. Tappitt. Business made it needful that he should be daily about the brewery, and there occasionally he met the poor departing man wandering among the vats and empty casks like a brewer's ghost. There was no word spoken between them as to business. The accounts, the keys, and implements were all handed over through Worts; and Rowan found himself in possession of the whole establishment with no more trouble than would have been necessary in settling himself in a new lodging.

That promise which he had half made of sending bridecake to Mrs. Sturt before Christmas was not kept, but it was broken only by a little. They were married early in January. In December Mrs. Rowan came back to Baslehurst, and became the guest of her son, who was then keeping a bachelor's house at the brewery. This lady's first visit to the cottage after her return was an affair of great moment to Rachel. Everything now had gone well with her except that question of her mother-in-law. Her lover had come back to her a better lover than ever; her mother petted her to her heart's content, speaking of Luke as though she had never suspected him of lupine propensities; Mr. Comfort talked to her of her coming marriage as though she had acted with great sagacity through the whole affair, addressing her in a tone indicating much respect, and differing greatly from that in which he had been wont to catechise her when she was nothing more than Mrs. Ray's girl at Bragg's End; and even Dolly had sent in her adhesion, with more or less cordiality. But still she had feared Mrs. Rowan's enmity, and when Luke told her that his mother was coming to Baslehurst for the Christmas,—so that she might also be present at the marriage,—Rachel felt that there was still a cloud in her heavens. "I know your mother won't like me," she said to Luke. "She made up her mind not to like me when she was here before." Luke assured her that she did not understand his mother's character,—asserting that his mother would certainly like any woman that he might choose for his wife as soon as she should have been made to understand that his choice was irrevocable. But Rachel remembered too well the report as to that former visit to the cottage which Mrs. Rowan had made together with Mrs. Tappitt; and when she heard that Luke's mother was again in the parlour she went down from her bedroom with hesitating step and an uneasy heart. Mrs. Rowan was seated in the room with her mother and sister when she entered it, and therefore the first words of the interview had been already spoken. To Mrs. Ray the prospect of the visit had not been pleasant, for she also remembered how grand and distant the lady had been when she came to the cottage on that former occasion; but Rachel observed, as she entered the room, that her mother's face did not wear that look of dismay which was usual to her when she was in any presence that was disagreeable to her.

"My dear child!" said Mrs. Rowan rising from her seat, and opening her arms for an embrace. Rachel underwent the embrace, and kissed the lady by whom she found herself to be thus enveloped. She kissed Mrs. Rowan, but she could not, for the life of her, think of any word to speak which would be fitting for the occasion.

"My own dear child!" said Mrs. Rowan again; "for you know that you are to be my child now as well as your own mamma's."

"It is very kind of you to say so," said Mrs. Ray.

"Very kind, indeed," said Mrs. Prime; "and I'm sure that you will find Rachel dutiful as a daughter." Rachel herself did not feel disposed to give any positive assurance on that point. She intended to be dutiful to her husband, and was inclined to think that obedience in that direction was quite enough for a married woman.

"Now that Luke is going to settle himself for life," continued Mrs. Rowan, "it is so very desirable that he should be married at once. Don't you think so, Mrs. Ray?"

"Indeed, yes, Mrs. Rowan. I always like to hear of young men getting married; that is when they've got anything to live upon. It makes them less harum-scarum like."

"I don't think Luke was ever what you call harum-scarum," said Mrs. Rowan.

"Mother didn't mean to say he was," said Mrs. Prime; "but marriage certainly does steady a young man, and generally makes him much more constant at Divine service."

"My Luke always did go to church very regularly," said Mrs. Rowan.

"I like to see young men in church," said Mrs. Ray. "As for the girls they go as a matter of course; but young men are allowed so much of their own way. When a man is a father of a family it becomes very different." Hereupon Rachel blushed, and then was kissed again by Luke's mother; and was made the subject of certain very interesting prophecies, which embarrassed her considerably and which need not be repeated here. After that interview she was never again afraid of her mother-in-law.

"You'll love mamma, when you know her," said Mary Rowan to Rachel a day or two afterwards. "Strangers and acquaintances generally think that she is a very tremendous personage, but she always does what she is asked by those who belong to her;—and as for Luke, she's almost a slave to him."

I won't say that Rachel resolved that Mrs. Rowan should be a slave to her also, but she did resolve that she would not be a slave to Mrs. Rowan. She intended henceforward to serve one person and one person only.

Mrs. Butler Cornbury also called at the cottage; and her visit was very delightful to Rachel,—not the less so perhaps because Mrs. Prime was away at a Dorcas meeting. Had she been at the cottage all those pleasant allusions to the transactions at the ball would hardly have been made. "Don't tell me," said Mrs. Cornbury. "Do you think I couldn't see how it was going to be with half an eye? I told Walter that very night that he was a goose to suppose that you would go down to supper with him."

"But, Mrs. Cornbury, I really intended it; only they had another dance, and I was obliged to stand up with Mr. Rowan because I was engaged to him."

"I don't doubt you were engaged to him, my dear."

"Only for that dance, I mean."

"Only for that dance, of course. But now you are engaged to him for something else, and I tell you that I knew it was going to be so."

All this was very pretty and very pleasant; and when Mrs. Cornbury, as she went away, made a special request that she might be invited to the wedding, Rachel was supremely happy.

"Mamma," she said, "I do love that woman. I hardly know why, but I do love her so much."

"It was always the same with Patty Comfort," said Mrs. Ray. "She had a way of making people fond of her. They say that she can do just what she likes with the old gentleman at the Grange."

It may be well that I should declare here that there was no scrutiny as to the return of Butler Cornbury to Parliament,—to the great satisfaction both of old Mr. Cornbury and of old Mr. Comfort. They had been brought to promise that the needful funds for supporting the scrutiny should be forthcoming; but the promise had been made with heavy hearts, and the tidings of Mr. Hart's quiescence had been received very gratefully both at Cornbury and at Cawston.

Luke and Rachel were married on New Year's Day at Cawston church, and afterwards made a short marriage trip to Penzance and the Land's End. It was cold weather for pleasure-travelling; but snow and winds and rain affect young married people less, I think, than they do other folk. Rachel when she returned could not bear to be told that it had been cold. There was no winter, she said, at Penzance,—and so she continued to say ever afterwards.

Mrs. Ray would not consent to abandon the cottage at Bragg's End. She still remained its occupier in conjunction with Mrs. Prime, but she passed more than half her time at the brewery. Mrs. Prime is still Mrs. Prime; and will, I think, remain so, although Mr. Prong is occasionally seen to call at the cottage.

It is, I think, now universally admitted by all Devonshire and Cornwall that Luke Rowan has succeeded in brewing good beer; with what results to himself I am not prepared to say. I do not, however, think it probable that he will succeed in his professed object of shutting up the apple orchards of the county.